Penguin Books
The Abramsky Varia

Morley Torgov's previous book, *A Good Place to Come From*, was a Canadian bestseller, winning the coveted Leacock award for the best book of Canadian humour published in 1975.

The Abramsky Variations is Torgov's first novel. He lives in Toronto where he is a practising lawyer.

Morley Torgov

The Abramsky
Variations

Penguin Books

Penguin Books Ltd, Harmondsworth,
Middlesex, England
Penguin Books, 625 Madison Avenue,
New York, New York 10022, U.S.A.
Penguin Books Australia Ltd, Ringwood,
Victoria, Australia
Penguin Books Canada Ltd, 2801 John Street,
Markham, Ontario, Canada L3R 1B4
Penguin Books (N.Z.) Ltd, 182–190 Wairau Road,
Auckland 10, New Zealand

First published in Canada by Lester and Orpen Limited 1977
First published in the United States of America and Great Britain
    by Penguin Books 1978
Published in Canada by Penguin Books 1978

Made and printed in Great Britain by
Richard Clay (The Chaucer Press) Ltd,
Bungay, Suffolk
Set in Linotype Baskerville

For Anna Pearl, Sarah Jane and Alexander

For their advice, help and encouragement, special thanks to Beverley Slopen, Helen Mathé, Harry Olch, Marvin Cohen and the Ontario Arts Council

Paris, May 21, 1927: *Colonel Charles A. Lindbergh, of the United States of America, today became the first person in history to fly across the Atlantic Ocean. Taking off from Roosevelt field, Long Island, at 7:52 a.m. yesterday in his single-engined monoplane "The Spirit of St Louis," Colonel Lindbergh landed at Le Bourget Airport, outside Paris, at 10:00 p.m. this evening. On hand at the airport were thousands of wildly cheering Frenchmen who had waited hours to greet him. France's President tonight hailed Lindbergh's feat as one of the most significant in the annals of human achievement. "Colonel Lindbergh has constructed an aerial bridge between the old world and the new," declared the President. It is expected that the aviator will return to New York City and a hero's welcome unprecedented in that metropolis' history.*

One

Charles A. Lindbergh never knew this, but Leibel Abramsky did:

On that day in May, 1927, at the very moment Lindbergh's aircraft was bouncing across the field at Le Bourget, Abramsky's shoes were shuffling down a gangplank at Halifax harbour. Both voyagers – one alone in his dark cockpit, the other crammed like an anchovy into a steerage-class dormitory – had just crossed the Atlantic for the first time.

The two men never met. In fact, Lindbergh never knew Leibel Abramsky (or Louis Brahms, as he soon chose to call himself) existed. But for the next fifty years of Abramsky-Brahms' life, scarcely a day passed that wasn't affected by the spirit of Charles Lindbergh.

The relationship began with Abramsky's change of name.

Abramsky was a violinist. Born in Kamensk-Podolsk in the Ukraine, he made his way to Rumania after

7

Russia's hospitality ran out. There he found work in the heady little cafés of Bucharest, playing not only for his supper, but for breakfast and lunch as well. Eventually his Rumanian hosts began making pointed and rather sour comments about his tendency to second helpings and the numerous lumps of sugar he took in his tea. When that occurred, Abramsky knew it was time to pack up his fiddle and push westward.

His train wasn't more than a dozen miles out of Halifax when he decided that "Leibel Abramsky" was hardly a suitable name for a musician seeking employment in the new world. Why not, you ask? After all, what is so North American about "Jascha Heifetz" or "Mischa Elman?" If "Jascha" and "Mischa" could be lived with, surely band leaders and audiences could accept "Leibel Abramsky" without difficulty or embarrassment. But the truth was that Abramsky was no Heifetz or Elman. Though he was in his late twenties and had been playing the violin since early boyhood, any child prodigy of the times could have fiddled circles around him with one hand. Aware that he lacked virtuosity, Abramsky felt that more doors would open to him if his name was at least easy to pronounce. He resolved to change it, and as soon as he stepped off the coach at Toronto, where friends had recommended he settle, he chose "Louis" as a replacement for "Leibel," conveniently inspired by the plane that had recently borne Charles Lindbergh into fame. That was progress in America.

"Abramsky" became "Brahms" at the suggestion of a clerk in the City Hall where Abramsky went to see about becoming a naturalized citizen. ("Brahms," said the clerk, "is a perfect name for a musician. Everybody will think you're related.") The musician's instinct about his change of name, and the clerk's instinct too, for that matter, proved correct. Before long Louis Brahms became known for his inexhaustible repertoire of Yiddish songs and dance tunes, all of which he played, if not brilliantly, at least energetically and

8

with feeling. Engagements to play at weddings, bar mitzvahs and parties of all sorts began to pile up, and Brahms was obliged to install a private telephone for himself when the landlady of his rooming house complained that he was monopolizing hers. That, too, was progress in America.

In the autumn of 1928, Abramsky was hired by Morris Glicksman, a prosperous baker, to play at the bar mitzvah of Glicksman's youngest child. "This is my big sister," the boy said, introducing Goldie Glicksman to the musician during an intermission. For the rest of that evening Brahms played everything by heart, fastening his eyes not on his sheets of music but on the fulsome young woman of twenty-two who danced to every traditional Jewish tune as if the old country was in her blood.

Courting Goldie Glicksman was no easy challenge. Her father, though he had arrived barely twenty years earlier from Poland, was unenthusiastic about having a recent immigrant – and a violinist at that! – as a suitor for his daughter, and made it clear by his cold manner every time Brahms came to call. Still vivid in Glicksman's memory were musicians who sat all day in outdoor cafés in his native Warsaw, sunning themselves and eating delicacies bought with borrowed cash. Goldie's mother hoped for a doctor or lawyer. Her brothers secretly made fun of Brahms' broken English, imitating his Russian accent so accurately that Goldie, though she tried not to, laughed aloud. Nevertheless, Goldie found the violinist more and more attractive. Perhaps it was his blond hair, gray eyes, and fair skin that made him look more Russian, more dashing, than the dark-haired, dark-eyed young dandies who frequented the Glicksman parlour. Perhaps it was his vocation, a far cry from professions that were generally acceptable in her parents' sight, and more romantic certainly than totalling a column of figures or pressing a stethoscope to a chest.

9

If Goldie's parents lacked geniality as hosts, the hostelry and its surroundings were even less inviting. The Glicksman residence was located directly over the bakery and could only be reached by a stairway at the rear of the shop. Brahms was thus required to pass under the critical eyes of a shop full of neighbourhood gossips whenever he paid a visit to the young woman upstairs. Once in the apartment, the challenge was to secure a few square feet of peace and orderliness. Usually this was impossible. The three Glicksman sons filled every chair and table with their scribblers and text books. They could quarrel for a solid hour over the ownership of a gum eraser. Often such disputes were settled only when one or other of the senior Glicksmans came bounding up the stairs from the shop to order the disputants out of the house.

Privacy, therefore, was almost out of the question in that household.

And outside, on the sidewalks of Baldwin Street, the atmosphere was no more conducive to trysting. The pavements were thick with merchants and customers haggling with each other. Wooden crates were stacked everywhere. Between the slats of some of the crates, chickens stared out, like prisoners on death row, condemned to the ritual slaughterer's blade, yet surprisingly stoic. Other crates held fruits and vegetables and smelled of crushed wine-grapes or damp celery. Barrels of garlic pickles competed with barrels of vinegar for control of the air around the entrances of the grocery stores. In many of the shop windows, cats sat resting, storing energy for the nighttime when men slept and mice came out to play their own desperate survival games.

All these circumstances might well have discouraged others, but not Louis Brahms. Brahms was a professional immigrant. Many times before, doors had been slammed in his face, welcome mats had been hastily withdrawn, suspicious glances had been cast in his direction. All these things and many more had happened to him in Russia, in Rumania, even on board the hellish old ship that brought him to this side of the ocean. He had endured it all. Perhaps because of it, every sunrise was to him as miraculous as the birth of a baby. In his soul he was convinced that, while all men were born to die, some men were born to live, and he was one of that blessed legion. Whenever Goldie complained about the bedlam in the apartment, or the bedlam in Baldwin Street, Louis would grin. "Goldie, you don't know what bad is. Thank God you never will."

In defiance of wretched accommodations and the opposition of everyone around her, Goldie saw more and more of Louis Brahms. Even Goldie's employer, a member of the provincial legislature to whom she was secretary, discouraged her. "You're an educated young woman; you want someone who can offer you all the good things in life," he would say, perhaps thinking of himself. His name was Andrew MacInnis. A bachelor, MacInnis was in his early forties. His chambers in the legislative block assured the visitor that the MacInnis family had been in the land since before Confederation and that in all likelihood he himself would be in office for as many years as it pleased him and God. The oak desk at which he worked had belonged to his grandfather; one of the first Scottish settlers north of Lindsay, and publisher of a small weekly newspaper. The leather chair in which he sat had belonged to his father, a renowned physician. The walls bore photographs of his own graduating classes at Upper Canada College and Osgoode Hall, as well as a regimental picture taken in England in the spring of 1919, by which time he was a major with two years' service in France behind him.

The young Jewish stenographer from Baldwin Street had won first prize for speed and accuracy at business college. Her other award was a position with the distinguished legislator. "What do you think? My Goldie's working for a bigshot in the government," Morris

Glicksman would announce to his customers. Then, as if to allay certain inborn fears, his own as well as his customers', he would add quickly: "It's true he's a gentile, but he's a very fine man." At Christmas MacInnis presented Goldie with a generous bonus and on New Year's Day he invited her to accompany him to the Lieutenant-Governor's levee at Queen's Park. "Your Excellency, may I present Miss Gladys Glicksman, my friend and secretary ..." After the introduction, "Gladys" Glicksman of Baldwin Street had drunk a glass of punch – her first ever – and bitten into a dainty ham sandwich – also her first ever. A drop of punch had landed very noticeably on her white blouse, and the thin slice of ham tasted rubbery and salty. The young Jewish woman retired in embarrassment to the ladies' washroom to cover the stain with a cloth flower, and rinse out her mouth. Studying herself in the mirror, the prizewinner at stenography awarded herself nothing more than a passing grade for her debut in high society. She swore to do better next time ... if there were a next time. She prayed there would be.

For the time being, however, she was more comfortable – there was no denying it – in the company of Louis Brahms.

"You still seeing that greenhorn fiddle player?" MacInnis would query from time to time.

"Yes."

"What do you see in him, anyway?"

Goldie Glicksman wasn't sure what she saw in him. Not yet, at any rate.

One day, when MacInnis posed this question, Goldie thought for a moment. To MacInnis' astonishment she replied, a bit hesitantly: "I see ... I see Charles Lindbergh ..." Others who put the same question to her were dumbfounded by the same response. Her closest friends told her she was out of her mind.

And perhaps Goldie Glicksman *was* out of her mind. But if she was, she was not alone. Reporters pursued Lindbergh everywhere, emptying their dictionaries onto the printed page with daily accounts of his every move for the benefit of wide-eyed readers; photographers, when they couldn't take pictures of the great aviator himself, took pictures of clouds, birds, anything that would remind the insatiable viewer of the miracle of flying; poets and philosophers rhapsodized about the symbolic significance – man risking his life against nature, and winning; and the clergy saw in Lindbergh yet another example of God's wonderful will. In Lindbergh's honour mankind created new weather phenomena – tickertape blizzards and confetti showers. Never before had a hero evoked such mass adulation.

In short, the whole world was out of its mind.

Goldie had begun to keep a scrapbook about Lindbergh soon after the landing at Paris and the Glicksman household was under strict orders not to dispose of a single newspaper or magazine until she had combed its pages for suitable material. On Louis' visits, they would sit at the diningroom table, she cutting and pasting, he smiling indulgently and waiting anxiously for ten o'clock when Papa Glicksman and his wife and the three boys would take themselves off to bed. Alone at last, the violinist and his winsome Canadian girl could hold hands and steal kisses.

Louis' passion, like his violin playing, was energetic, intense, and, alas, of less than virtuoso quality. In an embrace his lips pressed too hard so that they seemed to attach themselves to, rather than touch, hers. His hands, rather than fondling her breast or buttock, became possessory, as if staking a legal claim to a territory rather than enjoying an excursion. As a lover Louis Brahms was a little too much like a starving man unearthing a scrap of food.

Despite his handsomeness, she felt imprisoned within his arms, smothered by his ardour. Unable to free herself physically, Goldie instead unlocked her mind and made believe that the man crushing her against him was Charles Lindbergh. Only then did it all become palatable, even exciting. As his advances grew more intimate, she found that she could bear her submission best by allowing her thoughts to slip out from under, to roam freely, even wildly. The more the violinist's hands worked to arouse her, the less she was able to distinguish between her sincere and her make-believe impulses. She felt that she should pause to reflect, to analyze her thoughts, but somehow there was never the time (for he was always there, pressing) and never the talent (how could she concoct answers when the questions themselves were so nebulous?): Trusting that some form of alchemy would eventually render this union perfect, she gave herself up to Louis Brahms, pretending all the time to see and feel more than was in reality at hand, pretending to be – with Lindbergh!

The violinist and the baker's daughter were married on a fine Sunday afternoon in April, 1929. Ambitious now not only to give his new bride all the good things in life, but to prove himself to her parents (who wept under the canopy throughout the entire wedding cere-mony), Brahms formed "Louis Brahms and his Melody Makers," a group of six musicians. Before long, the Melody Makers had enough bookings to carry them comfortably into the following year.

On nights when the Melody Makers were engaged, Goldie would stand in the hallway of their small apart-ment watching Louis put on his coat and hat, holding his violin case, clasping it to her bosom as if it were a child and handing it to him when he was ready to leave with a kiss on his cheek. "Go, my Charles Lindbergh," she would say as he went out the door. And she would imagine that for the next four or five hours her hus-band, though he wore a trim-fitting coat and a fedora and not a leather jacket and riding breeches like Lind-bergh, *was* Lindbergh.

So much in demand now were Louis and his Melody Makers that Glicksman was forced to admit that his initial distaste for the young violinist from Russia was a mistake. His son-in-law had proved as solid and reliable as a loaf of rye bread. In a moment of largesse, Glicksman promised the young couple a new Essex for their first anniversary. Louis declined politely. "No thank you, I'll buy a car myself as soon as winter's over." The baker pretended to be hurt, but inwardly he was pleased, very pleased.

It was during the long days and nights when she awaited the birth of her first child that Goldie began her second scrapbook about Charles Lindbergh.

Almost from the beginning of her pregnancy, she complained of nausea and backaches, and these conditions became so severe that she was forced to abandon her plan of working right up to her confinement. To her parliamentarian's regret – he embraced her over and over again on her final day in his employ – she retired to her small apartment to live the life prescribed for expectant mothers. She knitted; she sewed; she made a point of cooking hearty breakfasts for her husband even though the sight of eggs in the morning made her ill. As for knitting and sewing, she might as well have handled the needles with her toes; everything she made had to be ripped apart. "Don't fret," Goldie's mother soothed. "We'll buy whatever the baby needs."

Eventually her flaccid attempts at domesticity vanished. She took to staring out of the livingroom window at the trucks and cars clattering by on the street below, at the pedestrians rushing to catch streetcars, at children skipping along the sidewalks to school. Everyone was going somewhere – everyone but Goldie Brahms. She looked up at the sky from her window and thought: that same sky must be visible over New York, over London, over Paris. Paris! Where Lindbergh had landed. Paris, where Lindbergh had been bathed in champagne and love; where he had been enshrined in a hotel suite usually reserved for royalty, had slept in a gold-draped room, feasted on the finest food in France, received Europe's richest and noblest citizens. She was there with him, with Charles Lindbergh, in his bed, at his table, on the balcony overlooking the

Champs Elysées, accepting the adoration of the crowd on the street below.

Goldie lost herself completely in her scrapbook. Soon she filled the second, began a third, filled it and began another. Louis, arriving home late at night after an engagement, would find her asleep on the livingroom floor next to her piles of magazines and newspapers, her scissors and her paste pot. Awakening with a start, she would cry out: "Charles?" Louis, a loving man, would reply quietly: "No Goldie, it's only me, and I'd like a cup of tea, if you can manage it."

Manage that much she could, and did. But little more. Between her upset stomach, her back pains and her scrapbooks, there was little time for anything else in Goldie's daily schedule.

Even the October stockmarket crash on Wall Street made no impression upon her; it was as if a meteor had bitten into the earth's crust somewhere in far Afghanistan; it simply had no significance as far as she was concerned.

Her father moaned over the demise of his mining stocks and decided against expanding the bakery. Her brothers worried that they might not get to college if things became worse.

When his bank withdrew its financial support, Louis was forced to lay aside plans to rent his own dancehall and start up an entertainment and catering business. He began to feel himself reeling; the platform under him teetered as he played; the people dancing on the floor seemed to be shuffling blindly toward the centre of a whirlpool.

"The world is coming to an end," he whispered, afraid to say it aloud lest the surface of the earth should rip open at the sound of his words. For the first time since he set foot in the country, lines of fear spanned his forehead.

"Think of Lindbergh," Goldie would say. "Think of his courage; his loneliness in the face of uncertainty and danger."

"Don't make speeches to me about Lindbergh," Louis would reply. "I'm choking to death, and you talk to me of Lindbergh."

As the first gray months of the Depression wore on, Louis withdrew into his own anxiety, Goldie into her own fantasy. In response to her husband's misgivings about the future, Goldie constantly urged him to consider the great aviator. "Only think of Lindbergh," she repeated time and time again, an expression of dreamy faith in her eyes.

He wondered if he had wedded some foolish child, and his impatience with her grew. Still, at night he would girdle her large belly with his arm and fall asleep aching for her.

The birth of their son occurred on the eve of their first anniversary. Instead of the Essex promised by Morris Glicksman, there was a cheque for three hundred dollars. It was the last substantial gift the young couple would receive from the baker. Glicksman's holdings had amalgamated with the general ruins of the times. He was reduced to doing what he had done in the first place – standing over a long table kneading loaves of dough.

By the spring of 1932, little Hershy Brahms was a thriving two-year-old. For his second birthday the boy received from his father a red tricycle with white wheels. Goldie bought two pictures, one of Lindbergh in the uniform of a colonel of the United States army, the other of his plane, which she hung over the boy's bed.

Louis Brahms and his Melody Makers were now reduced to a trio – Louis, a sad-looking clarinetist, and an accordian-player with holes in his shoes. Meanwhile, Goldie Brahms was completing her sixth scrapbook of Lindbergh memorabilia.

Returning from work – what little work there was – Louis would often find Goldie and the boy on the floor of their tiny livingroom poring over the pictures in

17

the scrapbooks. "See, airplane, air-*plane*," Goldie would say, pointing to Lindbergh's silver craft.

The boy would attempt to repeat it: "Eh-pane."

"No, not 'eh-pane,' say airplane!"

"The kid's soaking wet. It would do him a lot more good if you'd change his diaper," Louis would say. To advice such as this Goldie turned a deaf ear. "Try it again," she would say to Hershy. "Say like mommy says: Lind-bergh air-plane."

One evening, Louis was summoned to the telephone. The caller, a prominent poultry wholesaler, spoke with a gruff Russian accent. "Brahms," he said, "I'm cancelling the original plans for my daughter's wedding. Sorry, but we gotta cut down a little. Times are tough. All we're gonna need is a piano player. Sorry, Brahms, but you know how it is."

"But . . . but we had a contract . . ." Louis was fuming.

"So sue me," the caller said, and hung up.

Turning from the telephone, Louis caught sight of his wife and son engrossed in pasting into the latest scrapbook a picture of the Charles Lindberghs and their recently-acquired estate in New Jersey.

Wounded by the caller's callousness, needing in turn to inflict wounds, Louis shouted at the two: 'I wish your goddamn scrapbooks would burn in a fire!" The child screamed, and for a week afterwards Goldie refused to share Louis' bed. He begged her to return. "Please Goldie," he pleaded, "I was upset. Life seems to be one cancellation after another.'

"Go tell it to your chicken dealer," she said, cancelling yet another of Louis' expectations.

After that incident, barely a word passed between them until the night Louis arrived home brandishing a headline in the evening paper. "You see, Goldie," he shouted, "this is the price of fame." Goldie read the headline: "LINDBERGH BABY KIDNAPPED."

"Look at it, Goldie. Cut it out. Paste it in your book," Louis said. "You still want to be a Lindbergh?"

Goldie wasted no time. Though every penny counted

(thank God Morris Glicksman owned a bakery; at least the Brahmses always had bread on the table), she hastened to the neighbourhood variety store and purchased not one, but two, thick scrapbooks.

Taking note of these purchases, Louis said, a strong note of disapproval in his voice: "You're expecting maybe a shortage of scrapbooks?"

Goldie ignored the question. Indeed, she gave no sign that she knew the questioner was even alive. In neat, large letters she printed on the cover of one of the new scrapbooks "Charles Lindbergh – Book No. 7." On the first page she pasted the headline, an ugly foreword to what became over the next months an album of one man's misery. Page after page was filled with Lindbergh's anguish, every detail recorded with inhuman attention. Louis looked on, incredulous that in a world crumbling on all sides, his wife was consumed with this one calamity.

One night Louis' accordian-player failed to show at a wedding where they were to perform. The following morning a pair of shoes with holes in them was found, together with a shabby black dinner jacket and a black bow tie, on the edge of a wharf at the foot of Bay Street. The accordian-player's body was found several days later.

"The police are sure it was suicide," Louis said to Goldie. "Anyway, it couldn't be murder. Poor men don't get murdered. It's their one advantage in life."

"They found the Lindbergh baby today," Goldie responded. "Dead, poor thing. Poor Lindbergh."

"Goldie, my accordian-player's dead!" Louis looked into his wife's eyes, wondering whether or not they saw anything at all in that room – including him. "Do you hear me? He's gone. My rotten luck!"

"So much suffering," Goldie said, turning her eyes away. "Months of waiting, hoping, torture ..."

Louis was yelling now: "For Godsake, Goldie, I'll have to start all over again. Find a new man. God knows where."

19

Goldie's eyes focused on her husband just long enough for her to say: "The world's full of people who can play the accordian."

"Do you know what it means to break in a new man? To teach him all my arrangements? The last one – may he rest in peace – took weeks and weeks."

She wasn't listening. She was hundreds of miles away in the livingroom of a large country house, near Princeton, New Jersey, sharing the grief of Charles Lindbergh, comforting him, pressing his head against her bosom.

The new accordian-player didn't work out. He was a temperamental fellow who had once led his own orchestra in Vienna – or so he claimed – and was not about to take directions from any fiddler from the Ukraine. His successors, an Italian and a Pole (Jewish accordianists were now temporarily out of stock), were unable to blend their musical origins with Brahms', and each had to be let go. Demoralized, the clarinetist gave Louis a week's notice, and, almost overnight, Louis Brahms was a one-man Melody Maker.

The only market open to a solo violinist was the small inexpensive wedding ceremony, a humble affair held in second- and third-storey apartments with a handful of guests and a few bottles of homemade wine put up for the occasion by the groom's father. Of music there was little: a sentimental old-country tune or two as the family and relatives assembled; "Here Comes The Bride" as the maiden, looking out-of-place in her flowing white gown, made her way carefully along the narrow aisle separating "his side" and "her side;" and "The Wedding March," launched into with as much gusto as a solo violin can generate the moment the groom's foot had crashed through the tiny glass placed for that very purpose on the floor. Those few who had good taste gave Louis his fee in a white envelope; most of the time he was handed his few dollars out of the host's pocket in the hallway at the top of the stairs, as he was leaving, as if he were a delivery boy.

Going to work was itself a solitary business. Goldie

no longer held his violin case while he put on his coat and hat. There were no farewell kisses blown to each other as he went out the door.

"I'm going now."

"All right."

"I won't be late. They just want the usual."

"I know."

"You'll be here when I get home?"

"Where else will I be, Paris? What a crazy question."

"Will you still be up?"

She didn't reply. That was a crazy question too. Of course she would still be up. Up with her scrapbooks. Up too in the sky, seated next to her aviator.

"Goodbye then. I have to go."

"Go, Charles Lindbergh, go."

Once upon a time she had spoken these words to Louis as though he were himself The Lone Eagle and she his princess urging him to greater and greater heights. Now there was only irony in her voice, as if she had come across him at the foot of a cliff, lying on the stones, his wings broken and useless, a ridiculous dying bird that never learned to fly.

By the time Bruno Hauptmann was apprehended and imprisoned, awaiting trial for the kidnap-slaying of the Lindbergh baby, Louis Brahms found himself in a prison. To make a living he was forced to help out in the Glicksman bakery. Old Morris wasn't sorry to have his son-in-law in the business. His own sons showed no inclination to help their father. The eldest, Max, was on his way to becoming a lawyer; the other two prayed for admission to medical school (though, if necessary, all three would have joined the Foreign Legion – anything – to get away from the heat of the ovens and the shrill old Jewish women who elbowed each other in the lineups to get the first loaves Friday afternoons).

Working at Glicksman's bakery by day, playing violin nights and Sundays as often as he could, Louis

Brahms managed to keep three meals a day on the table. The gold he had expected to find in the streets of Toronto took the form of staple groceries handed to him from the shelves of the bakery by a creaking father-in-law. "Here, take home a jar of jam for Hershy," the old man would say, reaching up with a groan, pushing it across the counter at Louis with another groan, as if the jar contained his last life's blood.

One beam of light shone in Brahms' existence — Hershy. The child turned out to be uncommonly bright. Spurred on by Goldie, he learned to read before he entered kindergarten. "Lindbergh's airplane" no longer presented difficulties for the boy.

"Read for daddy," Goldie would say.

And the child, stumbling only occasionally at some extraordinarily long word, would read in a firm clear voice: "The Supreme Court today con-si-dered the last des-per-ate appeal by att-or-neys for Bruno Hauptmann, the con-vic-ted kid-napper due to be ex-e-..."

"Executed."

"Ex-e-cu-ted ..."

Louis would frown. "This you give him to read, Goldie? Kidnapping? Executions?"

Goldie would fetch a letter from the morning's mail and hand it to the child. "Here, Hershy, your father prefers you to read *his* kind of news." And the boy would read:

"Dear Mr. Brahms. I'm sorry you weren't paid yet for the wedding music but my father says if my in-laws refuse to pay like they were supposed to, then he will pay something on account next month around the first ..."

Not long after Hauptmann's execution, by which time Goldie, with as much aid from Hershy as his childish limits would allow, had compiled nearly a dozen swollen scrapbooks, Louis pointed to the latest Lindbergh headline. "LINDY AND WIFE LEAVE TO TAKE UP RESIDENCE IN ENGLAND."

"Some life," Louis said. "A man can't even have a

little peace in his own home. Three years since that kid was stolen and they won't let him alone. To England he has to run away."

"They won't exactly be living there like shleppers, you know," Goldie said.

"You think they want to run away to a foreign country?"

"England's not so foreign. Russia I call foreign. But England, no. It'll be like a second home. I envy her."

"Her" was Anne Lindbergh, seldom, almost never mentioned by Goldie.

"What's to envy?" Louis asked.

"What's *not* to envy?" Goldie replied. "A rich famous man for a husband; handsome, influential. They'll live like a king and queen there. You like it better the way we live?"

Louis looked at her in disbelief. "We've got our son. He's alive for Godsake. Don't you think Lindbergh would give anything just to get his kid back? If somebody called him up and said to him 'Mr. Lindbergh I've got your baby but it'll cost you your big house, your money, your medals, everything,' don't you think Lindbergh would gladly sign all of it over, every damn bit of it?"

Goldie was silent.

"Well, don't you?" Louis insisted. "Wouldn't you, if you were Charles Lindbergh?"

Where do the answers to such questions come from? From the heart? The mind? From both? Not always. Sometimes answers come from a worn-out linoleum in a room that serves as kitchen and diningroom and livingroom. They come from cracked plaster in the ceiling; a toilet that constantly overflows; an icebox that leaks; a sofa that has to be covered with a blanket and doilies to conceal rips and stains.

An accordian-player has taken his life? The world is full of accordian-players. Lose one, find another.

A child is kidnapped and slain? The world is full of children. Lose one, make another.

Louis persisted. "Goldie, dammit, I'm talking to you. Wouldn't you give up anything to have your own flesh and blood given back?"

"If I were Lindbergh?"

"If you were Lindbergh?"

"No."

Goldie reached for the newspaper. "If you're finished with this, I need ..." As her hand touched the front page, Louis brought his fist down hard, pinning her fingers just as she was about to draw the paper toward her, and causing the page to tear in a jagged diagonal line.

Goldie screamed: "Idiot! Now look what you've done." Louis assumed he'd broken her fingers. He hadn't. He had, however, ruined the front page of the newspaper. The Lindbergh item was bisected, which was probably as bad, if not worse, than broken fingers.

"Now I'll have to get another paper," Goldie cried. "Another five cents. Five cents we can't afford. Brute. Idiot."

"Then you'll give it up, damn you. You'll give up this craziness once and for all." As he said this, Louis headed for the bedroom closet where Goldie stored her precious library of scrapbooks. Goldie screamed again: "Oh my God!" Running after him she caught his arm as he reached up to the stack of scrapbooks on the closet shelf. She dug her fingernails as hard as she could into his upraised wrist making him gasp with the sharp pain. He swung around as she clung to the arm, and attempted to fling her away but she hung on and succeeded in pulling him a few steps from the closet. Only then did she let go.

"Whore!" he spat at her. "Lindbergh's whore. I'll burn your lousy scrapbooks if it's the last thing I do."

"Go ahead. What difference will it make? You'll still be Leibel Abramsky. You've lived like a greenhorn, you'll die a greenhorn." She repeated: "Greenhorn!"

In a house in Kent, with a splendidly overgrown garden, the Lindberghs settled comfortably. The year was 1936. Anne Lindbergh's father, once an ambassador, had family connections in England and Wales, and the Lindberghs, for the first time in years, enjoyed shelter from the unsleeping public eye.

The Brahms family, to economize, moved in with Morris Glicksman and his wife in an apartment over the bakery. Old Glicksman was now too arthritic to knead dough, and it was all his wife could do to pick up a dozen rolls and deposit them in a paper bag without dropping one or two on the floor. His oldest son was clawing his way through Osgoode Hall, earning three dollars a week as an articled student. The other two Glicksman boys were struggling in the inhospitable climate of the University of Toronto Medical School, financing themselves with part-time jobs wherever they could find them. For the benefit of her sons, Mrs. Glicksman established and maintained a scholarship fund that was fairly typical for the times; she pawned and unpawned and pawned again every ring, bracelet and necklace in her meagre inventory of jewellery.

And there was another important source of revenue on which the Glicksman boys had come to rely – Louis Brahms. He ran Glicksman's Bakery by day, assisted by a baker who had recently emigrated from Poland and who, fortunately, thrived on hard work.

Louis still managed to pick up engagements to play at weddings and bar mitzvahs but, like all things in life, even this simple occupation began to present complications. The familiar old-country tunes could be played solo, and people hummed or sang along, and clapped their hands in time with the music, content to be accompanied by a single instrument. But what about up-to-the-minute hits? Louis' more sophisticated clients now called for Irving Berlin tunes, and songs from *Porgy and Bess*.

Of course Louis was familiar with Berlin's and Gershwin's songs. But play them solo? Impossible. One needed a pianist, a drummer, perhaps even a saxophone to harmonize and carry the melody through one

25

or two choruses. That meant organization – arrangements, sheet music, temperaments to deal with.

"I don't know what to do," Louis said to Goldie. "The old stuff isn't enough anymore. They want foxtrots; they want rhythm. They want I should play like Paul Whiteman. I don't know what to do."

"Do whatever you want," Goldie said without lifting her eyes from the front page of the newspaper.

She was engrossed in an account of Charles Lindbergh's first visit to Germany.

Louis decided then and there.

The next morning he spoke to the baker from Poland. "Yoshke, you're a good worker. You work hard."

"Hard, yes."

"And you're clean."

"Yes, clean, yes."

"And steady."

The baker nodded yes.

"And I think you're an honest man."

The baker blushed. "I try," he said.

"I'm gonna take you in on a deal, Yoshke. You want to be a baker all your life, or a boss?"

Without hesitation, Yoshke answered, grinning: 'A boss."

"Okay then. You and me are gonna take this bakery and turn it into a *real* business!"

The idea was this: instead of selling their bread and buns to coffee shops in the area, Louis would rent the vacant store next to the bakery and convert it to a coffee shop. It could be done cheaply. A few pieces of used furniture would do for a while. They could produce fresher pastries for their coffee shop patrons, and more cheaply. The local competition would be no match at all for this oven-to-table operation.

Old Glicksman fretted. "It's no time to be putting your name on a lease, buying tables and chairs, cups and saucers!"

The two future doctors fretted. If Louis' plan failed, bankruptcy would surely follow.

Goldie scolded her husband for almost an hour, scarcely pausing to catch her breath. "Since when are you a businessman? When's the last time you ran a restaurant? Or were even in one? When you were in Russia maybe? Or in Rumania?" On she went, convinced in her own mind, and attempting to convince him, that he had no talent whatever for what he was about to try.

Only Max Glicksman, the oldest of the Glicksman sons, encouraged Louis. Having received his call to the bar, Max had squeezed himself and a few law books into an office on Dundas near Bay Street not much larger than a clothes closet and was anxious to promote business. "Tell you what," he said to Louis. "Old man Brenner owns that empty store. I've know him since I was a kid. If I can put together a good deal for both of you, I'll get a fee from Brenner, and as for you, my dear brother-in-law ..."

Louis interrupted. "But I haven't got money to pay you a fee."

"From you I'll take a partnership interest. I'll gamble. If it goes well, I get twenty percent of the profit. If it goes under, I get nothing. Fair enough?"

"Fair enough."

Max Glicksman had learned his lessons at law school well. Brenner was delighted to rent the store for little more than the sum necessary to pay the taxes and insurance on it. And Louis was equally delighted. "I never thought I'd be able to rent it so cheap," he exulted to Max. "I got it – how do you say? – for a song."

"That's the story of your life, Louis," Max said. "All your life you've gotten something for a song."

Not quite. Old Glicksman was obliged to hobble into the bank to sign a note for his son-in-law's loan of two thousand dollars. His fingers, with their swollen knuckles, trembled as he scrawled his signature on the line over the printed word "Guarantor." And that night there was hell in the aparment over the bakery.

27

Mrs. Glicksman rocked back and forth in her chair moaning that her husband had signed away his life at the bank. The medical students called Louis a schemer and an opportunist.

To be sure, Goldie was on hand to add to Louis' troubles. "So, hero, are you content now? You've tied up my father hand and foot with this idea of yours. That's what you had in mind all along, isn't it?"

"What are you talking about?"

"You can't make a go of anything. So you have to see to it that everybody around you fails too."

Louis shouted at his wife: "I don't understand. You wanted me to think like Lindbergh, to act like Lindbergh."

"Fool!" she shrieked. "I wanted you to *be* Lindbergh."

Glicksman wailed. "Crazy. She's crazy." The two future doctors agreed on the diagnosis: they were quite positive Louis had driven their sister insane. Goldie's mother moaned and rocked. "We're all crazy," she said. "There's a devil in our lives, that's all there is to it."

Max Glicksman, who had ridden out the storm from a safe chair in a corner of the room, calmly rose and called to Hershy: "Come Hersheleh, Uncle Max is gonna buy you a Popsicle. In fact, Uncle Max is gonna spend all the money he made today and buy two Popsicles. One for you, one for me."

They sat on a wooden crate outside Drapnik's Dairy. Their tongues brushed the frosted flanks of the Popsicles.

"Uncle Max?"

"Hm?"

"What does she mean about Lindbergh?"

"Someday maybe we'll find out. Eat your Popsicle. It's running down your fingers."

"Uncle Max?"

"What now?"

"Are you ever gonna get married?"

"Me?"

The boy looked up at his uncle. "Are you ever gonna get married?"

"Hell no!"

Within a year, Glicksman's Hearth-to-Table Coffee Shop had become a small magnet attracting not only customers from the immediate vicinity but from neighbouring districts as well. At first, the steadiest patrons were folk with unorthodox timetables: poultry dealers who rose at dawn with their roosters, policemen who walked their beats late at night, and cab drivers who never seemed to sleep at all. Then, an intern from the General Hospital discovered the coffee shop and before long the tables were occupied by young men in white cotton jackets jabbering excitedly about first appendectomies. Lawyers and businessmen followed, some coming from as far away as Bay Street to eat chopped egg on a fresh onion bun. Louis paid off the original bank loan, and borrowed another three thousand – this time without his father-in-law's backing. The new loan was put to good use: glass-topped tables and chairs with padded leatherette seats were purchased, a tile floor of black and white checkerboard squares was laid, an electric sign lit the front window, and old-fashioned bins were replaced with gleaming showcases. Yoshke, who ran things in the bakeshop, was at last a boss; two assistants were hired to work under him. Glicksman's Bakery was now a round-the-clock operation.

In October of 1937 Louis, Yoshke and Max Glicksman made a unanimous decision: they would open a second location.

Again there was a scene in the apartment, but this time Max Glicksman acted as a staunch and vociferous advocate for Louis. Again Goldie scolded. "We're just getting on our feet. Now you're going to throw away what little we've got."

That night, after Hershy was asleep, Louis said to Goldie: "We're moving. I'm going to look for an apartment. Something close, only a couple of blocks away."

"And how will we pay rent?" Goldie asked. "How will we furnish it? With what?"

"I'll sell my violin if I have to. I'll do anything. But we are moving, do you hear?"

"But I'll be cooped up with Hershy," she protested. "I'll never be able to get out, not even for a minute. At least here ..."

"You'll have your beloved Lindbergh to keep you company," Louis said. "As a matter of fact, here's the latest item for your library."

He tossed a newspaper across the bed in her direction. She pressed its front page flat on the blanket and read a headline in the lower section: "LINDBERGH RECEIVES GERMAN DECORATION FROM GOERING."

"You see," Louis said quietly. "Yesterday, the darling of Broadway. Today, the darling of the Wilhelmstrasse. The Fuehrer's pal. You must be proud of him, no?"

Next morning, before leaving for work, Louis said to Goldie: "Where's last night's paper? I want to see if there's a nice apartment for rent somewhere near here."

Goldie pointed in the direction of the garbage pail under the kitchen sink.

When Louis extracted the newspaper from the garbage, he was surprised to find she hadn't touched the front page. The Lindbergh story was there, without so much as a line snipped out. The only change in the page was a large amber stain, left there by some coffee-grounds.

By the summer of 1938 one of the favourite topics of conversation among Louis' customers was the apparent love affair between Charles Lindbergh and Germany's political leaders. The mutual admiration that shone in photographs of Lindbergh and certain Luftwaffe generals convinced Louis, like most readers of the papers, that the man called The Last American Hero might indeed turn out to be just that. After all, if this was the road American heroes chose to travel, then who needed American heroes?

Louis began to wonder about Goldie. He noted that,

while the daily papers, and especially the Jewish press, were full of Charles Lindbergh's encomiums about the German Air Force, Goldie's scissors had gone cold and the rubber applicator on the top of her bottle of glue had become crusted through disuse. Apart from a single innocuous column about the Lindberghs' move to France, Goldie selected nothing to insert in her current scrapbook. When rumours appeared in print of a further move by the Lindberghs – this time to Berlin – Goldie threw the newspaper into a refuse bin. The disposal of a daily paper was no longer a matter of grave economic concern to Goldie Brahms.

In April, 1939 the Lindberghs returned to America and an icy reception from a press that only a few short years ago had invented new superlatives to fit the legend. Lindbergh was now preaching an unpopular sermon, a message that seemed to have been written for him by the Nazi Minister of Propaganda himself: Germany had fighting superiority; let other nations engage in the suicidal business of challenging that superiority; as for America, she must isolate herself, remain neutral.

Louis said nothing to Goldie about her idol's steady fall from grace. There was no need to; the papers recorded the descent of Lindbergh's star as assiduously as they had recorded its sudden and irresistible ascent twelve years earlier. Editorials labelled the aviator pro-Nazi and called upon the United States government to revoke the honours it had once bestowed upon him with such love.

Before the end of that summer, Canada was at war with Germany. On the morning war was declared, Goldie Brahms went to Hershy's bedroom (Hershy now had his own bedroom, as well as a porch to play in, in a lower duplex apartment located in the north end of the city near Bathurst Street); without a word she removed the photographs of the Colonel and his aircraft which had hung over the boy's bed, in one apartment or another, since his second birthday.

She sat at the edge of Hershy's bed, holding the pictures in her lap. She saw her aviator putting on his coat and hat, checking himself over in a full length mirror, making certain that his wing collar and black bow tie were properly centred. She heard voices – hers, his, echoing as if in a high-ceilinged chamber.

— Where are you going, Charles?
— I told you – General von Holtzmann is giving a dinner at the Officers' Club.
— Must you go? Every night lately it seems—
— I'm late Goldie. We'll talk about it in the morning.
— But why can't I go? The other men take their wives whenever ...
— I said we'll talk about it in the morning.

She is alone, standing before the full length mirror. Her hair is too black, her large eyes are too brown and heavy-lidded, her lips too full, the skin of her face too sallow. It is a face that will never do at von Holtzmann's table. Frau von Holtzmann is seated at one end of the long table. To her right sits Charles, dutiful, attentive, pretending to be fascinated by his hostess' description of last summer's closing performance of *Tristan und Isolde* at Bayreuth. All around the dinner table polite German is heard ("Sie wissen ... Sie machen ... bitte, nehmen Sie ..."). There is the comfort of belonging; blue eyes look into other blue eyes, fair skin blends easily with blond hair; the men sit erect, their bodies stiffly at attention even as they eat, bending their close-cropped heads ever so slightly to make a chivalrous response to a lady's inquiry; the women whisper through crisp discreet lips. Nothing – *nothing* – is in excess here. Suddenly the double doors of the private dining salon are thrust open and Goldie appears. She wears a long black dress and a white fox around her neck. General von Holtzmann, who stands at the head of the table proposing a toast to "Unser amerikanischer Freund Herr Lindbergh," stops in mid-sentence. Even the bubbles in his tulip-shaped champagne glass have frozen in place. Everyone turns to face Goldie, glaring at her. Someone whispers: "It's the Jewish woman ..." Goldie lets out a sob, turns and flees ...

The dream was over. There was nothing left except the shame, and that, too, was confused, for now Goldie saw herself running a gauntlet. On one side stood old Morris Glicksman and his wife pointing swollen, arthritic, accusing fingers at her, wailing: "You have lain with a goy, with a friend of Goering to boot!"

Their accusations, their tearing of hair, meant nothing to her.

It was, rather, the hostile narrow blue eyes on the opposite rank of the gauntlet, the eyes of General and Frau von Holtzmann, that aroused in Goldie the deepest feelings of shame. Goldie's lips had never felt fuller, her skin sallower, her hair blacker. She dared not meet those eyes with hers.

Sitting there on the edge of Hershy's bed, Goldie Brahms knew she had committed the worst sin of all for a Jew – the sin of being ashamed to be a Jew.

Louis watched her wrap the pictures in brown paper and tie them with twine.

"What're you doing that for, Goldie?"

"Never mind."

The pictures disappeared.

On the first day of Chanukah that year there was a celebration at the apartment over the bakery. Max Glicksman raised his glass and proposed a toast: "Let's drink not just to another new coffee shop; let's drink to a whole chain of coffee shops!" Everyone drank. Everyone but Goldie.

"You're not drinking, Goldie?" Max said.

"You know I don't like liquor," she snapped.

On the following morning the third coffee shop opened for business. Louis personally escorted the first patrons to their seats. Discreetly, Max Glicksman left his professional card with four important dress manu-

33

facturers who were wolfing down early morning bagels in one corner. Yoshke, who was now every inch the boss (his bakery assistants swore he counted every poppy seed that fell to the floor), showed up a half-hour late that morning, grinning sheepishly. For the first time in years, he had slept in.

Louis Brahms took stock.

Lindbergh's fortunes had fallen; his own had risen. And yet his relationship with Goldie, instead of warming, as he expected it would, remained distant. If anything, the abyss between them grew wider and deeper. Goldie seemed totally curtained off by melancholy, a state from which she emerged for only a few minutes nightly when she sat with Hershy after supper reading to him or listening to him read from *Black Beauty* or *The Adventures of Toby Tyler*. Louis would return late from his small office at the bakery and drink his nightly cocoa in silence. In the darkness of their bedroom they lay, he facing one wall, she the other, without touching, talking about the boy.

"Hershy read for you tonight?"

"Yes."

"How much?"

"A lot."

"How much is a lot?"

"A whole chapter."

"He read good?"

"Perfect. He read 'Constitutional Government' for the first time, and without a mistake."

"Maybe Sunday I'll get a chance to hear him read. Good night, Goldie."

"Good night."

The family doctor called it "a case of nerves." For this he prescribed pills to help her rest. "Get some help in the house too," the doctor advised Louis. "She needs to take things a little easier."

They hired a maid, Mary Yurchuk, who came three

days a week to clean and cook and to whom Louis spoke Ukrainian.

The pills seemed to make Goldie more restless. Different pills were prescribed. They helped her sleep but she awoke dazed and nauseous. She spent hours seated at the livingroom window staring at her reflection in the glass.

The family doctor called it "depression" now, and prescribed pills to pep her up. She took to pacing the livingroom floor in the middle of the night.

Louis could say nothing to her that didn't arouse ire, contempt, hostility.

"Do you want to go for a little ride in the country?"

"When, next year?"

"Of course not next year. Sunday."

"Who knows where I'll be next Sunday."

"Why do you talk like that, Goldie? You make it sound as if we're all going to fall off the earth."

"We did that a long time ago."

Louis began driving Mary Yurchuk home when her day's work was done. The cheap cotton housedresses she wore couldn't conceal the strong full curve of her hips. Her bosom announced itself immediately whenever she entered a room. Though muscular, her legs were white and straight. Her body gave off an intoxicating amalgam of smells – perspiration, garlic, some kind of lilac-scented lotion that she used on her face. Despite the unromantic tools of her trade – galvanized pail, mop, wax polish – she displayed a certain coquettishness. At Louis' inquiries into her love-life (she had lived for a time with a Croatian taxidriver, now in jail for assaulting a rival for her affection) she laughed girlishly. Bending over her pail, reaching under a table to get at a difficult corner with her scrub-brush, she was conscious of Louis' eyes on her and, glancing at him over her shoulder, scolded him in Ukrainian, pretending to be indignant. They laughed, but discreetly, for while Goldie understood no Ukrainian, she understood laughter.

Indeed, Goldie, who found so little to smile or laugh about, understood this laughter all too well.

"I had to let her go," Goldie announced one evening to Louis.

"But why?"

"I caught her stealing."

"Stealing! I can't believe it. What did she steal?"

"Ask her. She knows what she took."

The new cleaning woman was a taciturn Finn who grunted as she rubbed and polished, looked neither to left nor right, and came and went in silence.

In Mary Yurchuk's room, in a boarding house in Parkdale, Louis asked: "What does she think you stole?"

"Don't you know?" the young woman giggled.

"No."

"Then you're blind, Mister."

They made love on Mary Yurchuk's bed. "Easy, *easy!*" she whispered as he forced himself into her before she was ready. The bedspring squeaked and creaked with an urgent rhythm, excitedly, as if it too were an active participant in the lovemaking. Afterward, taking leave, Louis deposited a small stack of new ten-dollar bills on her night table. "Here," he said, "get rid of that mattress. And get yourself some curtains."

"Oooo, so much money!" she cooed, arranging the bills like playing cards in her hand.

"I can afford it," Louis said. "Just fix this place up. I want it to look . . . nice."

With the United States' entry into the war, Charles Lindbergh, it seemed, had nothing more to say to America; at least nothing America cared to listen to. Had Goldie Brahms been of a mind to maintain an up-to-date scrapbook, she would have been hard put to find material. For the time being, Lindbergh's star had disappeared from the sky.

But Louis' star, as far as Goldie was concerned, was

still nowhere to be seen in the heavens. The opening of another coffee shop, the construction of a larger bakery, the purchase of a fine two-storey brick house, a good solid navy blue Chrysler in the garage – none of these things brought Louis alive in her eyes. She seemed to accept the trappings of Louis' financial success – a fur coat, the house, the car – with a kind of anger, as if she were being entombed in them.

Old Glicksman died; she wept perfunctorily at his graveside. Soon after, her mother followed; again there were barely any tears. The two younger brothers became physicians and went overseas with army medical units; it was as if total strangers had gone off to war; she bade them goodbye without so much as a sniffle.

Her mind was now a collection of cobwebs that had somehow indurated to form an impassable barrier. Whatever light managed to filter through – and it was meagre even at the best of times – emanated from Hershy. From her son she could still take pleasure. A precocious twelve-year-old, he wrote poetry (which Louis had him copy in neat letters for proud public display in the office of the bakery) and could perform at least a half-dozen Mozart piano sonatas by heart on the new mahogany upright that had joined the Brahms family the same week as the blue Chrysler.

Hershy was the only ground upon which Goldie and Louis Brahms met.

"You're the only person I can talk to," Louis said to Max one day. "I don't understand what has happened. Lindbergh becomes a nobody. And all of a sudden, it's as if I've become a nobody too. One goes, and – poof! – the other also disappears. How can it be? She's your sister, Max. Do you understand her?"

Max, still a bachelor, with more business now than he could handle, shrugged. "Women," he said.

Hershy found the package under the front seat of the Chrysler; a small, flat tin box with a picture on the lid of an Arab mounted on horseback against the backdrop of an orange desert. Inside lay three tightly-curled circles of white rubber. He had never seen them before.

"Where did you get them?" Goldie asked. He held the tin box in the palm of his outstretched hand, innocent, looking up at her pale, threatening face.

"In the car."

"Give them to me," she ordered.

Late that night Hershy was awakened by voices from the kitchen.

"I got them at the drugstore, where else?"

"What for?"

"What do you mean 'what for'? For us. What else?"

"Liar! Since when have we needed them, or anything for that matter?"

"I thought maybe ..."

Louis knew there was no point in finishing his sentence. He was plainly unconvincing.

"It's that Ukrainian bitch isn't it?" she cried.

"So, you had Charles Lindbergh all these years."

"I never slept with Charles Lindbergh."

"What's the difference?" Louis said. He put on his hat and coat and left the house, slamming the door behind him.

The bakery was, of course, pulsating with late-night activity when Louis drove up.

"What are you doing here so late?" Yoshke called. "Even *I'm* going home. It's been a long day."

"I'm sleeping here tonight," Louis answered.

"Here?"

"Here."

Yoshke understood. "Women," he said to himself.

It was less than a week before Hershy's bar mitzvah, the night Goldie Brahms died. Or took her life. No one was quite sure which pills did it, the yellow ones that were supposed to make her sleep, or the pink ones that were supposed to keep her awake. At the cemetery, Hershy stood wrapped in Louis' arms repeating the mourner's kaddish, and as they walked from the field

Max Glicksman walked with them, his hand gripping Hershy's. Behind them, close by, walked Yoshke, and behind him a long line of people, all speechless, all looking bewildered.

And why not? They had just buried a shadow. Flesh and blood, and bones too; and yet, a shadow.

On the night of Goldie Brahms' funeral, after the solemn dutiful callers had departed, after the cellophane-wrapped fruit had been rewrapped in preparation for tomorrow's visitors, after Hershy had gone off to bed (with cheeks sore from the well-meaning pinches of fond uncles and aunts), Louis Brahms lay awake in bed. His eyes followed a long slender swordblade of light that sliced across the ceiling, reflecting from a streetlamp. His nostrils took in the scent of fresh bedlinen, and the faint odour of a bottle of Shalimar on the dresser – the last bottle of perfume he'd bought for his wife. He ran his fingers across his chest and shoulders, down along his stomach, between his legs, around his hips and thighs. He touched his knees.

"I'm alive," he thought. *"Alive!"*

On the night of Goldie Brahms' funeral, the spirit of Louis Brahms took wing at last. And flew.

May 25, 1969: Thor Heyerdahl, with a small crew, today set sail aboard the papyrus-reed boat "Ra" from the northwest coast of Africa headed in the direction of an Atlantic current he hopes will carry his craft westward to the Indies. The journey may prove that thousands of years ago Egyptians managed the same trip in the same way. How else, Heyerdahl reasons, can one explain the existence of pyramids on the Sahara and in the distant jungles of Mexico? Will "Ra" withstand high winds and pounding waves? Will its primitive quarters and equally primitive provisions, designed and supplied to meet ancient standards, support modern men throughout the arduous months that lie ahead? Only time will tell.

Two

1969. A Monday morning late in May. Hershy Brahms sat at his desk making a prodigious effort to breathe calmly. An inner pressure threatened to explode in the middle of his body. He began to pray: "Oh Lord, our God, King of the Universe, grant me intestinal peace."

Up to this point the day had been difficult enough. On the Don Valley Parkway, in morning rush-hour traffic, the fuelpump in Hershy Brahms' practically-new Mercedes retired from active duty without so much as an advance "Achtung!" And when the tow truck arrived nearly an hour later it lacked the prescribed equipment for hoisting a vehicle of such rare and delicate breed. While Brahms waited for a second tow truck he re-read a report in the morning paper that Thor Heyerdahl and his crew, during the first hour of their departure from the harbour at Safi, had encountered a series of hair-raising mishaps that threatened to abort the voyage even before the green lowlands of Morocco had faded from sight. Yet, miraculously, the papyrus-reed craft had made it to the open sea. And here was Hershy Brahms, stranded in ten thousand dollars' worth of immobile metal on the shoulder of a six-lane racecourse, unable to complete the simple journey from his home in the suburbs to his office downtown. Brahms touched a button on the dashboard and muttered, "Well, at least *this* works!" as the sunroof slid back. Looking up at the sky through the open roof of his stricken sedan, he called out: "God ... it's me, Hershel Brahms, son of Leibel Abramsky. I demand to know ... were you around when they built this contraption, or don't you normally operate in the vicinity of Stuttgart? Do you realize I've just blown the better part of this morning and that I will never get a chance to regain the hours I'm wasting here? Has it occurred to you that Thor Heyerdahl will float all the way from Africa to North America ... *and back*! ... before I get to Richmond Street?"

The operator of the second tow truck finally showed up but insisted upon payment in advance when it was discovered that Brahms' motor league membership had expired. And at the repair depot, the white-coated service manager, smiling as recommended in Regulation No. 69-1-FP (for Fuel Pump), Customer Relations Manual, informed the distraught Brahms that the new part would be covered by warranty but not the labour or the towing charge.

And now, at his office, Brahms had just ripped his telephone (pastel green, a restful and calming shade according to his friendly Bell sales rep) from its wall socket, sent it clear across his desk, and watched it land on the floor some ten feet away where, despite the inch-thick pile of the broadloom, it broke into many calm, restful, pastel green pieces.

"Sonofabitch!" Hershy yelled, addressing the stack of files piled unevenly on the desk before him. "Son of a *son* of a bitch!" he repeated. The files responded by collapsing in sympathy, and spilling like a paper waterfall over the edge of his desk onto the floor, a gesture that only served to inflame Hershy more. Flicking his intercom switch he almost screamed: "Miss Harris, will you please get right in here." In an instant Miss Harris, with the face of a permanently terrified owl, was at his desk.

"Two things, Millie . . . Number One, don't ever put Jerry Gutspan through to me again without warning me first. Ever!"

"But I thought you'd be anxious to speak with him, Mr. Brahms. He's due in this afternoon with Mrs. Isaacs."

"I am never – repeat never – anxious to speak with, to, about, or around Mr. Jerry Gutspan."

"I thought since he's Mrs. Isaacs' accountant . . ."

"He is also her brain surgeon, her auto mechanic, her family counsellor, her TV repairman . . . In short, he's a goddamn grandstander and I loathe the sight and sound of him!"

"I'm sorry, Mr. Brahms," Millie said softly.

"Your apology's accepted," Hershy said, calming down. "Number Two, do me a favour, Millie dear, and get these goddamn files out of my sight."

Miss Harris looked at the files, then spotted the shattered carcass of the telephone on the carpet. She made a move, as if concerned first with picking up the bits of plastic and wire that lay at her feet.

"Never mind that," Hershy said. "Let the damn thing rot there. I'm going for a short walk, then to lunch. If Mr. Winston calls tell him I'll meet him as arranged."

Miss Harris looked at her watch. Timidly, she asked: "Will you be back by 2 : 30? Mrs. Isaacs and you-know-who are due then. You're supposed to be updating her estate plan, remember?"

Hershy looked thoughtful for a moment. "In case I never come back, Millie, tell Mrs. Isaacs I said to drink only bottled water, and look both ways before she crosses the street."

With that, Hershy Brahms strode out of his office

wishing that 2:30 would happen in the next century, on another planet. He knew that, promptly at 2:25, Mrs. Isaacs would be seated in his waitingroom. Cranky, semi-literate despite the hundreds of thousands of dollars Moe Isaacs had left her ten years ago when he fell (or jumped; the police weren't sure which) from the roof of his own apartment building, she would sit there, ignoring the handsomely-bound copies of *Horizon* spread on the coffee table. Instead, hidden behind her oversized sun glasses, lips pressed together, snapping her alligator handbag open and shut, she would think of ways to defeat the government, to hold onto what Moe had provided for her, asking her accountant if he had prepared all the statements for Hershy to examine. How she loved that expression "all the statements!" She hadn't the faintest notion of what it meant, but it had such an important, such an official ring. "I'll have Jerry prepare all the statements ... Will the government want to see all the statements? ... You go over all the statements, Mr. Brahms, and advise me what I should do ..." This was her contact point with business and bureaucracy: all the statements.

"Screw her, screw Jerry," Hershy muttered, leaving the lobby of his office building and walking into the Richmond Street sun. "But especially, please God, screw all the statements!"

Walking east along Richmond and turning south to Bay Street, Hershy Brahms saluted a brigade of fellow legal lieutenants on their way to various noonday appointments. Some were rushing to meet colleagues for a frenzied game of squash followed by a spartan container of cottage cheese, all suffered in the cause of physical fitness. Others would be meeting clients at private clubs to discuss fat subdivision agreements over thin consommé. Still others, like Hershy, would simply be seeking an hour's escape in a restaurant with an old pal.

One thing about Richmond and Bay, Hershy said to himself; there's always comfort in numbers.

44

Yes ... and no.

Unlike Brahms, most of the lieutenants were eager volunteers, men who knew well in advance of that first day at Osgoode Hall that the whole point of living was the call to the bar, the name on the letterhead, the annual tax-deductible conventions in Halifax and Winnipeg and Victoria, the Queen's Counsel after perhaps twelve or fifteen years of untarnished silver service to humanity and the incumbent provincial leadership.

The Brahms route had been much less direct. The six Mozart sonatas he'd learned to perform from memory at age twelve soon grew to the entire volume, to which Hershy added many more by Beethoven and Schubert. Chopin's études spilled effortlessly from his fingertips, and the subtle intricacies of Debussy and Ravel floated from the upright Mason & Risch like impressionist landscapes. At the same time, Hershy continued to write – poetry, short stories, articles for the highschool newspaper. At eighteen, facing college, Hershy auditioned for a Professor Di Silvestri of the Toronto Conservatory of Music. "My boy," said the Professor, "you have a nice talent. Enjoy it, nourish it. Play for your own enrichment, your family's, your friends'. But as for the concert stage, well ..."

The literary world was not ready for Hershy Brahms either. In his first year at the University of Toronto he submitted what he considered his finest piece in a short-story contest. The winner was a scraggly young Irishman who came from a farm near Chatham, whose clothes smelled like burnt porridge, and whose pen was tipped with genius. Hershy Brahms' submission rated a mere honourable mention.

Medicine? Rubber gloves and Vaseline? No, that was definitely out.

Engineering? Slide rules and beer parties? Not for your average Jewish boy in the late 1940s.

Law?

Naturally ... what else?

In the fashionable olde Englishe gloom of Cy's Rib

'n Bib, Hershy groped his way to Lenny Winston's favourite corner table.

"Where the hell have you been?" Lenny Winston half stood, extending his hand across the table to Hershy. Hershy shook Lenny's hand, at the same time catching the strong sweet scent of Canoe that Lenny patted onto his shaved face every morning by the cupped handful. Hershy sniffed the air, then winced more than was necessary. "Essence of Whorehouse?" he asked. He sat down, mouthing the word "martini" at the approaching waiter. The waiter, an expert lip reader, promptly about-faced and made for the bar. Lenny looked Hershy over, critically, the way a wine connoisseur examines a label. "You look kinda fuzzy around the edges, buddy," he said. "Bad day at Black Rock?"

"Why don't you stick to appraising real estate, Lenny,' Hershy retorted without rancour. It was customary for them to exchange small insults whenever they met. Occasionally, when they doubled with their wives for dinner, Hershy and Lenny carried on in this fashion, ridiculing each other's clothes, each other's cars, each other's aging physique, each other's diminishing sexual prowess, while Shirley Winston and Charlotte Brahms smiled tightly, letting their little boys have their little fun, wishing it would stop before they somehow became involved too.

Lenny continued to inspect Hershy. "I'm serious, Hersh," he insisted. "You do look a little less than your usual magnificence today."

Hershy gulped down the martini in a single draft. "Another," he called to the waiter, "and a plain omelette, no potatoes." Turning to Lenny again he said casually, not listening to himself: "So what's new Lenny?"

"Where the hell have you been? I tried to get you a few times over the weekend."

"This weekend was my nephew's bar mitzvah."

"So you blew Friday night and Saturday. But Sunday?"

46

"Heathen! On Sunday thou shalt serve Sunday brunch for the out-of-towners. Aunt Sadie and Uncle Ben from Detroit, some schmucky cousin with a Cadillac from Pittsburgh; blintzes, smoked salmon. Everybody asking, 'What's new? How's the kids? How's your car running? ...' Why were you calling me?"

"First to remind you of lunch today. Second because I had a nice little mortgage deal and I thought you might want a piece."

"That's not the kind of piece I had in mind over the weekend, Lenny baby," Hershy said, fluttering his eyebrows like Groucho Marx.

"Look Brahms, try pulling your head out from between your legs for a minute. Do you want a piece of the deal?"

"Is it good?"

"You sonofabitch," Lenny said good-naturedly, "I don't exactly go around peddling dreck, do I?"

Lenny Winston was one of the shrewdest money-men in town. On the outside he looked like an Arab captain, dark, handsomely fierce, a man who would have looked perfectly at home dashing across a North African desert on horseback, kicking up huge clouds of hot sand in the faces of his pursuers. Beneath the surface it was a different story. Lenny's soul was the Federal Mint, stamping coins, printing bills, churning dollars into thicker units of currency; churning day and night (Sundays and holidays included), living and dying with the rise and fall of dividends, interest rates and income taxes. But Lenny had integrity as well in his soul; even his detractors admitted that. His deals were clean and open, like bibles on church lecterns. Perhaps once upon a time he had cut corners, but with success and wealth had come probity. Lenny had even begun of late to use the services of Derek Hollenberg, the first Jew to become a partner in the prestigious law firm of McCarthy, Blake and Fraser, and one of the ablest corporation lawyers in town. "I'll have Hollenberg of McCarthy, Blake get in touch with you," Lenny would say whenever he was about to enter a deal. The other party to the deal inevitably got the message: the contract would go Hollenberg's way . . . or no way.

No, indeed, Lenny Winston did not go around peddling dreck these days. Still, it was unnatural in the relationship between Lenny and Hershy that this point should be openly and readily acknowledged. Quite the opposite. Hershy therefore answered as expected: "Winston, I've know you for damn near twenty years and I don't think you've learned the first bloody thing about mortgages. But go ahead and tell me all about your little proposition anyway. After all, *you* invited *me* to lunch. The least I can do is listen. What's the deal?"

"Small shopping centre. Brantford. Two hundred thousand second behind seven hundred thousand first. Coupla so-so chain stores and a supermarket. Rest all small independents but solid covenants."

"You like it?"

"I like it."

"How much is open?"

"I saved the last twenty-five for you."

"Short term?"

"Two years. One year closed. Thirteen percent . . . net to you, that is."

Hershy smiled knowingly. "Prick. How much you peeling off the top for yourself?"

"Up your ass, pal," Lenny smiled back. "I gotta Lincoln and a B M W to support. You want, or not?"

The offeree sat silent, pretending to think it over; that was part of the game – you never accepted a piece of a deal eagerly lest the offeror should think he was doing you a favour. Therefore, after the regulation pause, Hershy replied, with just the right tone of boredom in his voice: "I want, I want. I'll take twelve-five for me and twelve-five for Lou."

The word "Lou" was a light switch, lighting up Lenny's face. "Hey, how is old Lou?"

"Erect – as always," Hershy replied, beaming. He always beamed when he talked about Louis Brahms;

it pleased him to think about his father's unfailing manhood, gave him hope that he, the son, had been lucky enough to inherit what old Lou liked to call "Russian blood." "He's been in Israel for the past month." From the inside pocket of his jacket he withdrew several wrinkled sheets of airmail paper. "Here," he said handing them to Lenny, "you gotta read this."

Lenny, holding up one hand like a traffic cop, interrupted. "Please, spare me the details. I know the whole travelogue by heart. He's been to the Golan Heights, posed for a snapshot beside a captured Syrian tank, and knelt down and kissed the tarmac when he got off the plane at Lod. Right?"

"Right," Hershy said. "Also he planted a tree every hour on the hour no matter where he was. He even planted one in his hotel elevator. Now shut up and read the letter."

Lenny read:

Dear Hershy: What more can a person say about Israel? Israel is Israel and that's all there is to it. They made the desert bloom and in Tel Aviv and everywhere else even the police and the garbagemen and the hooers are our people, and when you go to cross the street or drive even around the corner you take your life in your hands because every day it's the same like Bathurst St. on Sunday only worse yet.

You remember I told you I got together with my cousin Moishe who now calls himself Zvi for some reason which he came originally from Odess and now lives in Haifa? Well he is driving me a hundred procent crazy and so is his wife who was born here a sabra and her name is Malka. They cant getover the fact that I never got married again after your mother (olive-asholem) died and they insist I have to meet every goddamn widdoe and old maid in Palestine, which it really does *not* hinterest me because they all go around like Malka with verykose vanes showing in theyr legs and theyr big fat bosoms hanging down like a bunch bananas. Feh! And they think they are so damn hindependant because some of them were in the army and can handle a gun like a real soldat! But who needs it. You

49

cant say 2 words to them because all they talk about is this country and how come if everybody is so rich in Canada we dont do more and come more often to Israel or even stay and live and marry them here, which its the last thing on my mind. Beleeve me Hershy if God willing Ill come back to Israel you can be sure I would *not* look up Moishe or Zvi or whatever the hell he calls himself because it proves that no matter where you go in this world (even Eretz Yisrool) you can locate a pain in the ass.

One night in Haifa I did manage to escape from Moishe and his wife the superman, and I went to have a drink in the bar in a hotel and it turns out that the casheer is a girl in maybe her 30s who was born and raised in Vancoover B.C. so natchurly she speaks English perfect. It turns out that she married an Israeli but theyre getting divorsed because he goes around doing crazy things all the time but the crazyest things of all he likes to do in the bedroom, and she thinks its all from when her husband was a prisoner of war in Syria. With all her problems she is still a very fine person and she made me feel more alive than anything else Ive seen in Israel.

Kiss Charlotte and my darling grandson for me and tell Yoshke not to forget our accountant wants all the statements in by the end of this month for those son-of-a-bitches in Ottawa in case I don't get back in time.

Your loving Dad

Handing the letter back to Hershy, Lenny chuckled admiringly, as if he had just watched from a ringside seat an aging bullfighter plunge his last sword between the horns of a panting expiring victim. "I bet there's more life in one of his balls than in all of yours and mine put together," Lenny said. "So tell me, how come he never ended up with another woman all these years?"

"Who says he never had another woman?"

"Well I thought ..."

"He had this Ukrainian broad for a couple of years, name of Mary Yurchuk. That was after my mother died."

"Really?" Lenny grinned, intrigued. He loved the thought of man and woman uniting premaritally, extramaritally, postmaritally – anything but maritally.

"Really," Hershy went on. "But then some nutty Croatian who'd been her lover and was doing two years for grievous assault came out of the clink and when he saw the posh setup Mary was living in, he knew she was being kept."

"So?"

"So he got sore and stabbed her to death. It took a couple of weeks for the police to find him and while he was on the loose my late Uncle Max got Dad out of town. They figured the Balkan terror might come after him with a breadknife too."

"Good old Lou," Lenny said with genuine admiration. "I never knew he was a man with a past. Is there more?"

"Oh, I think after Mary Yurchuk he used to shack up from time to time with the odd woman. But he was very discreet. As a matter of fact, I didn't know any of this until just a few years ago. When my Uncle Max was dying of cancer, he and I used to spend hours talking about Lou. I've never had the guts to confirm all those stories, but there's an old rule of evidence that dying men always tell the truth."

"But what about marriage? He must've wanted a companion, somebody to braise his shortribs?"

"Never. Out of the question!"

Incredulous, Lenny said: "Come on, there's gotta be somebody on this earth he's willing to share his precious body fluids with."

"Nope. You know, he goes to a lot of concerts. Every time there's some big-name violinist on the program he's there at the head of the line. Well, two years ago I arranged for him to spend a few days at Tanglewood. I think Menuhin was playing ... or was it Milstein. Somebody whose name starts with an M."

"Mantovani?"

"Sure Lenny, sure," Hershy said, patronizingly. "Anyway, while he was staying at this big old hotel in Lennox he met a Mrs. Wurtzberger."

"Mit de umlaut?"

"Nein, mit-out de umlaut, mit fistfuls of good green Yankee gelt. A real high-class German-Jewish queen mother from New York. Widow. Well-educated. Son and daughter both lawyers. First name was Eva but she pronounced it Ay-vah. Very classy."

"And a perfect momma for poor little motherless Hershy, eh?"

"Let me tell you, Lenny, all signs were go! After that meeting at Tanglewood she wrote him and invited him down to New York for the Labour Day weekend. So he goes to 'Nevyork' as he calls it, and it's hot as hell and Mrs. W. comes out onto her balcony and makes the fatal error of squatting down on a deckchair in her shorts with her knees a yard apart and her ankles together. And you know something? Old Lou suddenly remembers that his partner in Toronto has taken sick and he's on the next plane back, and Mrs. Wurtzberger goes up in smoke together with her education and her German background and her two beautiful lawyers and all her money."

"Too bad he's kind of over the hill. Boy, would he be a tiger in today's world." Lenny grinned again.

"Today's world? What's so special about today's world?"

Looking around him first to make certain no one could overhear, hooding his eyes to indicate that a confidence hitherto shared only with God was about to be revealed unto Hershy, Lenny bent across the table so close to Hershy that Hershy's fork was prevented from rising out of his half-eaten omelette.

"You wanna hear about today's world? Okay. Hot off the press. Guess what couple is making it with another couple," Lenny murmured.

"I knew you'd get down to the real business of the meeting eventually," Hershy said. "Okay, let me guess." Hershy raised his eyes ceilingward, searching the acoustic tiles for the answer, pretending to be vitally interested. "Give me a hint, Lenny. Do they deal in goods or services?"

Lenny looked petulant. "All right, you wanna be a smartass, I'm not gonna tell you."

"Aw come on Lenny, I was just kidding. Who?"

Lenny enjoyed playing hard to get. "Eat your heart out, Brahms." But Lenny couldn't keep up the pretence. Leaning forward into Hershy's face again he whispered: "Kenny and Greta ..." He paused for dramatic effect. "And Dick and Sandy Cobrin."

The Kramers and the Cobrins. Two of the most beautiful couples at the tennis club. Kenny Kramer, dress manufacturer turned builder and developer; Greta Kramer, who glistened as she walked sweatily off the courts and whose bathwater Hershy would gladly have bottled and stored in his basement, like vintage wine; Dick Cobrin, chartered accountant turned furniture tycoon who slept nightly with Sandy in a king-sized bed made to his personal specifications in his own plant; and olive-thighed Sandy who drove the male population of the tennis club right out of their shorts every time she bent down to pick up a tennis ball.

"It's got possibilities," Hershy admitted, "but 'Kenny and Greta and Dick and Sandy?' A title like that will never be big box-office."

"I don't think they're out to create pop art," Lenny said. "But the word is that they are having a helluva ball."

"You mean they're playing switch?"

"Better than that. They're switching together. Know what I mean? You ever try to imagine, Hershy, what it'd be like to ball your best friend's wife while he's balling yours and everybody's all together balling in the same room?" Lenny's eyes dilated, and his tongue covered the complete circuit of his lips in a gesture of delight at the concept just aired. "Think of it, old buddy," he continued. "I mean, that's real togetherness. Everybody doing it with everybody else's blessing.

No guilt. No hanky-panky. No phony bullshit. Right out there in God's great big wonderful wide-open."

"You make it sound like a movie about Texas," Hershy said. "However, pal, where I come from that's called crapping on your own doorstep."

"But how can it be?" Lenny protested. "It's what you lawyers would call a true joint and several venture."

"That's exactly what it is, Lenny, a venture. But that doesn't make it an *ad*venture, and there's one hell of a difference between the two."

"You're playing with words," Lenny scoffed. "The point is, it's something new, fresh, different."

"Okay, okay, I'm convinced," Hershy said, not in the least convinced. "Now, let's see you go charging home in your shiny silver Lincoln and convince Shirley."

Lenny lit a six-inch Romeo y Julieta and blew a thick first puff into the air. He searched the same acoustic tiles in the ceiling Hershy had searched earlier.

"Well, wise guy," Hershy prodded, "how do you think the little lady of the house will take to your brave new world?"

Lenny continued to scan the ceiling, but from the hundreds of tiny holes in the tiles not a single answer seemed to emerge.

No matter. Hershy knew the answer to his own question, because he knew Shirley Winston. They had met about twenty years ago at University College. Shirley was considered a prize catch; her father owned a chain of lingerie shops in Toronto and she wore cable-stitch tennis sweaters the cables of which strained to their woollen limits to contain her bosom. Shirley's father and mother had always dreamed their daughter would someday be carried off by a handsome young Jew who looked like an Arab Captain, and Lenny's parents, who operated a cigar store, had always dreamed their only begotten son would marry into some form of mercantile aristocracy. Lenny's kids – three boys – looked like junior-grade Arab Captains. The Winston house, which hugged two of the highest-priced residential acres in the city, was as close to an English country house as Shirley Winston could make it; none of your whites and golds and imitation French Provincial, but pale greens and yellows and plenty of genuine Hepplewhite and Regency installed by a darling interior decorator from Yorkville whose grandfather hailed from Minsk and whose aim in life was to mould all the Winstons of the world into Wasps.

Pursing his full lips as he blew rich clouds of Romeo y Julieta into the dark restaurant air, Lenny thought about Shirley. Shirley, sitting in the Temple sanctuary at their eldest son's bar mitzvah, fine chin held high but not too high, modestly, decently, virtuously; hair soft but sprayed with just enough lacquer to defy the irreverent Saturday morning winds of Bathurst Street, suit by Givenchy out of Creeds, wristwatch by Patek-Philippe (purchased fresh off the vine in Lausanne), small alligator clutchpurse, matching pumps ...

Hershy, knowing that Lenny was trapped, couldn't resist the temptation to paint his friend further into the corner. "You know goddamn well, Lenny, that you and Shirley couldn't carry on a routine like that if your lives depended on it. How long have I known Shirley, damn near twenty-one years, right? Do you know, every time we meet, say we go out to dinner together or we're at one another's house, whenever I go to kiss her hello she turns her head so all I get is a mouthful of hair? Honest to Christ, she does it every time. Like she's afraid maybe, if I kiss her on the lips, I'll suddenly shoot my tongue down her throat and bring it straight out the other end. That's Shirley, and you're full of shit if you think ole don't-touch-my-lips is gonna screw your buddy in front of an audience, the audience being you and your buddy's wife yet!"

Hershy studied Lenny's face intently after delivering this opinion, wondering: should I, or shouldn't I, ask what's on my mind? Then he decided what the hell. Carefully, he said: "Unless, of course, there's a side to Shirley I don't know about, Lenny ..."

"Shirley's great, honest Hersh," Lenny said. "She's really not as square as you think."

"But?"

"Well, it's just that she's – uh – a reactor. I mean, she'll do almost anything I suggest. We picked up this book in Amsterdam – I think I showed it to you one night – this book with all sorts of far-out stuff, pictures and all, and we've tried some of the stuff that's not too far-out. But I gotta do the suggesting. I gotta be the idea person. She never initiates anything. She's not an innovator, know what I mean? I just wish once she'd make the first move, that just once she'd grab me instead of my always grabbing her." Lenny's eyes were probing Hershy's now, trying to locate some small repositories of sympathy. "Don't you find the same with Charlotte?"

"I'll be honest with you Lenny," Hershy replied. "You might say that the phase of our sex life that concerns Charlotte most is the post-coital."

"I'm not a doctor. What the hell does post-coital mean?"

"I mean she is primarily worried about what comes after the come. To be specific, she likes to have the Kleenex immediately available, at the ready. That's the only way she feels at all secure. I'm lying there, gasping, trying to catch my breath and slow down my heartbeat, and all she can say is 'Get off, Hershy, and get me some Kleenex quick!' That's Charlotte's idea of afterglow. Anyway, the point is, Lenny, neither of us comes exactly equipped wife-wise to play your little game. You want to play mixed doubles at the tennis club with Shirley and Charlotte, okay; but that's about all you can hope for."

Lenny butted his cigar less than halfway through, crushing seventy-five cents worth of unsmoked Cuban leaf in the ashtray. "Hell, Brahms, there's got to be something more exciting to look forward to than whacking a ball across a net and going out for tea and a bran muffin afterward."

"Ah but there *is* something more exciting. There's—" Hershy broke off abruptly. He shrugged his shoulders, a sign that he had nothing further to say on the subject. Lenny eyed Hershy suspiciously, knowing that somewhere behind that shrug lay an interesting idea, an idea he was determined to root out.

"C'mon Brahms, this is no time for privacy. When you make that motion with your shoulders and stare into your coffee it means something is cooking in that brain of yours. Well?" Lenny smirked, knowing he was right, feeling wise and older-brotherly even though he was younger than Hershy by almost two years.

Hershy thought aloud, looking straight at Lenny as he spoke: "I don't know whether to tell you, or not. You've got the senses of a champion bloodhound when it comes to real estate. But when it comes to other things in life, sometimes you're a fuckin' brontosaurus."

Lenny should have been insulted but he wasn't. He loved being analyzed by Hershy, regardless of how brutal Hershy's observations were. It was a refreshing change from the dozens of real estate salesmen who lined up to embrace Leonard J. Winston's posterior; from the hardware and brick and lumber people he entertained in the summer at his farm in the Caledon Hills and who departed at two in the morning red-faced, bladders full of Lenny's Chivas Regal, waving cheery goodbyes and quietly, jealously praying behind their liquor-lounge laughter that Lenny would drown in his pool. No one on earth, not even Shirley Winston, could say to Lenny the things that Hershy said, and get away with it.

Glowing with affection for Hershy, Lenny said: "More, tell me more. I'm a brontosaurus, whatever that is, and unlike you I chose good looks in life instead of intelligence. But try me anyway, Hershy. Maybe, just maybe, I'll understand what you're trying to say. Only speak slow, you superior asshole."

"All right, I'll tell you. I don't suppose you saw that

news item on page three of this morning's paper, did you?"

"You know I always go right from the front page to the financial page. Who's got time for the garbage in between?"

"Well, amidst the garbage, as you call it, there was an intriguing piece about Thor Heyerdahl."

"Thor *who*?"

"Thor Heyerdahl." Hershy could see by the blank look on the handsome brontosaurus face that Lenny had never heard of him. "Christ, Lenny," he said, "you're gonna suffer an awful shock someday when you find out the Bolsheviks murdered the Czar and took over Russia. Thor Heyerdahl is this anthropologist from Norway who set out yesterday from the northwest coast of Africa in a papyrus-reed boat and he plans to sail in it and try to pick up a particular Atlantic current that'll carry him and his crew right to the West Indies. You see, his theory is that thousands of years ago the Egyptians managed to make it to the Western Hemisphere that same way. That's how come, according to him, there are these strange-looking pyramids in the jungles of Mexico. Just like the ones you see in the desert in Egypt."

Hershy paused, waiting for Lenny to express intrigue, or at least exhibit a mild interest in the subject of Thor Heyerdahl. Instead, Lenny sat staring impassively at his luncheon companion.

"Lenny," Hershy said quietly, passing his hand in front of Lenny's eyes like a hypnotist. Lenny blinked. "Go on Hershy," he said, "I'm still awake."

"I don't think you've heard a word I said, Winston," Hershy said. "I can see your mind is miles away, under the sheets with the Kramers and the Cobrins."

"I happen to have heard every goddamn word you just said. You want me to give it back to you, Brahms? Okay then, there's this Scandinavian nut by the name of Heyerdahl and, if he doesn't sink or get eaten alive by sharks or just rot to death in his papyrus Dixie cup,

58

he hopes to land in Mexico and uncover King Tut's putz under a pyramid in beautiful downtown Acapulco. Now will you please tell me something? What the hell has all this got to do with you? Are you Heyerdahl's lawyer? Is that the point?"

"The point, my brontosaurus friend, is that some men in this world manage to find real adventure in life. They ..."

Hershy halted, suddenly embarrassed by the unusual fervour in his voice. He wasn't used to speaking with anyone in such an urgent, almost passionate, manner, not even with so close a friend as Lenny Winston. Oh yes, in all the years they'd known each other, Brahms and Winston had indulged in moments of "true confession." Usually these followed events of defeat or disappointment: a Winston building scheme that began with great promise and overnight went gangrenous because some municipal department head insisted upon less land coverage here and an extra strip of greenbelt there; or a corporate merger on which Brahms had been doing the legal work for a whole year that ended in a broken engagement on the very steps of the altar. These events were like buying something high and selling it low – *precise* failures, and therefore easy to talk about notwithstanding the gravity of the losses. And in any event they always knew, Hershy and Lenny, knew as a matter of faith that they would recover, that there would be other building schemes, other corporate mergers. With absolute certainty they knew there would always be the excitement of packing for a weekend junket to Las Vegas, the excitement of taking delivery at the car dealer's showroom of the latest fruit off the assembly-vines. So what if you blew your brains out at the blackjack table? Next month's rental income would more than replenish the barren billfold. And so what if, among all the built-ins in the new car, there was also built-in obsolescence? Twelve months or twelve thousand miles from now you'd be eyeing the successor, picking your way through all the exotic options in the dealer's radiant catalogue.

But now it was different for Hershy Brahms, turning forty, and attempting for the first time to describe to his friend the germs of an *im*precise failure in his life as well as the possible antidote. A little friendly commiseration would simply not suffice here. No, Hershy Brahms' case required massive doses of understanding and sympathy. The question was: could Lenny Winston – eternally horny, eternally in search of life wrapped in bigger and brighter packages – be counted upon to fill the prescription?

Thus far, it seemed the answer was no. "Go on," Lenny said, still showing no sign of being enthralled by Brahms' vision of real adventure.

"Look. Lenny, I know I'm not making myself too clear. What I'm trying to get at is this: here is this guy Heyerdahl, who's already a successful scientist, and who could rest on his laurels and never bust his ass again, and he'd have all the fame and fortune he'd ever need. And what does he do? He stashes himself away in what you call a Dixie cup and takes a crack at floating across the whole goddamn ocean! Imagine that! He sticks his neck way out. Now look at me, at a guy like me, Lenny. What have I ever done? I'll tell you. I've managed to slice my way through life like a razorblade. You know what the characteristics of a razorblade are, Lenny? Thin, trim, clean ... and *no goddamn profile*. That's me Lenny. I've never once in all my forty years really laid anything on the line; never had to make a decision that could save my life or kill me, never been faced with a choice between freedom or prison, never once had to go out the door of my house in the morning wondering whether the day would end with a full belly or starvation. Even when I was a kid in the Depression, we always ate. All my roads have been paved for me; old Morris Glicksman spread the gravel, Lou poured the cement and Uncle Max painted the white lines down the centre. The only risks in my life are asterisks."

"I don't see what the hell you're complaining about, Brahms," Lenny said. "You and I, in fact most of our crowd, have been damn lucky in this world. We missed World War Two by a nose. We didn't get involved in Korea. None of us were nuts enough to bugger off to Israel and make like heroes. We managed to cash in during the greatest boom in history. Sure, we bitch and bitch and bitch about middle age and putting up with a lot of shit from our kids on one side of us, and our parents on the other side of us, and our wives on top of us, and the government crawling all over us like eczema. But you got to admit, pal, that it ain't exactly hell riding to work in a Mercedes and scooting off to your chalet in the winter and your cottage in the summer. Is it?" As far as Lenny Winston was concerned, the question was rhetorical.

Not so, however, as far as Hershy Brahms was concerned. "Toys, Lenny," he said. "All those things are toys. They're what we get for being good little boys and living like razorblades."

"What would you like society to hand out to you, then?"

"Ah, Lenny, that's exactly my point. Society can't hand out anything. Not any more. Don't you see, what I need I'm gonna have to go out and grasp for, tear out of the earth, or pull down from the sky. It's like starting fires by rubbing two sticks together; I gotta get the real feel of things."

"In other words," Lenny said, trying to suppress a smile, twitching his lips, "you figure the way to really get the feel of things is to become a caveman."

"Not exactly. I'm a twentieth century product and there's not a damn bit of use trying to escape that reality. What I want to be is a twentieth century man cutting through all the twentieth century crap of this world. Getting back to fundamentals. Know what I mean?"

"Sure. I can see you in a white loincloth growing your own wheat in your backyard, trotting over to the

61

shopping centre on your faithful donkey, walking barefoot to Miami every February." Lenny shook his head sadly. "I think, my friend, you've been seeing too many movies and too much TV. All that romantic stuff has gone to your head, that's what's wrong with you, Brahms."

Exhaling a hopeless sigh, Hershy reached across the table for the cheque. "I should have known anything less than fifteen percent per annum compounded half-hourly would be too subtle for you to understand, Lenny. Let me get the bill today." Hershy flashed a credit card in the air. The waiter, lurking in the garlicky shadows near a large wooden bowl of Caesar salad, came forward and plucked it from his fingers. "You should let me get it, Hersh," Lenny protested, "after all, I invited you to lunch." "Nonsense," Hershy replied. "It's been so refreshing being able to bounce my ideas off your head and reap the benefits of your keen analytical powers. Besides, I need the expense; the Income Tax Department's been complaining that I don't entertain enough."

Hershy made as if to rise from his seat, but was prevented from doing so by Lenny's firm hand on his arm, restraining him. "Look, Brahms, I'm not as big a schmuck as you think. I got some idea of what you're trying to say. You're not the only guy in the world who's restless, you know. But you gotta cut out all this back-to-fundamental bullshit and get back to reality. You remember the idea I had about getting into the condominium game? With your savvy, my dough, and our energy, we could make a fortune in the next few years. Christ, Hershy, you got a good twenty-five productive years ahead of you. How the hell do you want to spend it, in a papier-mâché canoe floating from continent to continent? Like Thor what's-his-name?"

"Poor poor Lenny," Hershy said, settling back in his chair. "You really think what you're doing is important, don't you? Let me tell you something, Lenny:

someday when my Mercedes is being lobbed across the Polish border in the form of a cannonball, and your Lincoln's being recycled into a dozen Pintos, some passerby is going to look at our names over the streaks of dog-piss on our tombstones and say 'Leonard Winston, Hershel Brahms, who the hell were they?' You, me, the rest of the blue suits in this room, we'll all be part of the earth's crust and nothing more. Your kids will tell their kids thrilling stories about how you developed a row of bungalows, and mine will tell theirs about how I saved a stupid bitch of a widow from paying her proper share of the federal debt when her rich husband kicked off. Big fucking deal!' "

This time it was Lenny who made a move to get up from the table. "You're depressing me, you bastard," he said to Hershy. "C'mon, we better get out of here. I'm sure you're anxious to pack and shove out to sea at high tide."

They walked out of the dark restaurant, blinking and shading their eyes in the bright two o'clock sun. "Thanks for lunch," Lenny said, offering his hand which Hershy took. "I'm sorry if I depressed you," Hershy said. "There's nothing more pathetic than a depressed brontosaurus."

Hershy walked Lenny to the parking lot, watched him hunch his tall frame into his polished silver Lincoln and roar off hot on the trail of a new shopping-centre site.

When Hershy Brahms returned to his office Miss Harris said: "Mrs. Brahms called from the animal clinic while you were out to lunch. She says the doctor says Herman has cataracts in both eyes. She said to tell you the operation will cost about two hundred and fifty dollars."

"Terrific," Hershy responded. "Call Mrs. Brahms back, Millie. Tell her to make sure the dog gets a private room."

Mrs. Isaacs was waiting for him. "Jerry'll be here in a few minutes. He's bringing all the statements," she said, eyeless behind her sunglasses, her lips slightly parted and pursed, waiting to ingest every single one of Hershy's precious pearls of legal wisdom.

A moment later Mrs. Isaacs and Jerry Gutspan were sitting opposite Hershy; two pairs of eyes dilated, two mouths opened wide, two fish just pulled from the water, sucking in the air of Hershy Brahms' office, sucking in advice, sucking hard.

Hershy glanced at his gold Rolex. Two-thirty, on the button. He was about to do what he was good at, what he was a regular ace at. Mrs. Isaacs and Jerry Gutspan were counting on him. His wife Charlotte was counting on him. So was his son Kevin.

Even Herman the Schnauzer was counting on him.

Late June. The parking lot at Yorkdale Shopping Plaza. Kevin Brahms, twelve, was about to depart with eighty-nine other kids for camp – eight weeks of Algonquin-Judaic culture costing heap plenty tax-paid shekels (in Hershy Brahms' tax bracket you had to earn two just to be able to spend one). Surrounded by gleaming Cadillacs and Jaguars and Buick station-wagons, two Gray Coach buses stood like patient cows, udders swollen with duffle-bags. A black Lincoln limousine, with a TV set built into the rear-section console, presided with sinister self-assurance over the assembly of vehicles. Mothers in crisp yellow or green sundresses, faces half hidden by oversized sunglasses, clutched to their bodies small fur-covered handbags that turned out on closer inspection to be Yorkshire terriers. (Charlotte would have clutched Herman, but he was still recuperating from eye surgery.) Fathers in French-made tennis shirts eyed each other's fraternal symbols – tiny embroidered alligators (in the sport-shirt industry eagles and lions were fast becoming extinct species). Hershy Brahms' wrist was weighed down by a heavy silver bracelet acquired during a rainy February afternoon in Freeport when there was nothing better to do. The camp assistant-director was shouting at the man who owned the Lincoln limousine: "We can't get the buses past your car, sir!" The man nodded imperiously to his chauffeur who backed up the Lincoln exactly three feet and not an inch more; a narrow victory for public transportation. Slapping his clipboard for attention, the camp director called out: "Okay, let's get this show on the road." Bus doors clamped shut, two diesel engines cleared their throats, gears began to grind. "Goodbye, goodbye ... write your grandfather ... wash your socks ... brush your teeth ... don't forget to use your Bug-Off ... write! ... we'll mail you stamps ... see you Visitors' Day ..." Kisses thrown through the tinted glass of the bus windows. Gasoline fumes. Bus exhaust. The two gray cows disappeared single file down the long parking lot, heading north to a sanitized wilderness in the northern Haliburton Highlands. Parents smiled, some with sadness, many with relief, and exchanged good intentions as they strolled to their cars ("We must get together soon for dinner ... Let's meet at the club for a game ..."). Oil stains on the parking lot asphalt. Yorkshire terrier pee stains. Last-minute gum wrappers ...

Ahead for Hershy and Charlotte lay July Weekend Specials.

Just Hershy and Charlotte at the cottage, childless, alone. Louis drove up to spend one Compulsory Sunday, bearing gift pickles and a long darkish wurst. Another Compulsory Sunday, Charlotte's parents underwent their annual lakeside endurance trials, complaining of mosquitoes, moving their canvas chairs every ten minutes to avoid sunburn, planning all afternoon how to avoid the evening traffic rush to Toronto, avoiding the remains of Louis' wurst, avoiding the water.

For the first weekend or two of every summer, Charlotte floated in a state of heightened sensuousness. She sunned herself on the dock almost in the nude, occasionally sneaking her shoulderstraps down and lowering her bra to the nipple-line when the neighbours were away, turning herself on at the end of the day by checking the tan on her smooth back and legs, drawing Hershy's attention to this, turning him on. But after that first couple of weekends, for some reason Hershy couldn't fathom, the current seemed to diminish. Once in a while she would run her hand, almost motherly, down the graying hair on his chest. Occasionally he would pat her behind, so neatly and tightly encased in her nylon swimsuit. Otherwise they seldom touched each other. Impassive, like a dermatologist conducting a clinical examination, he would take note of Charlotte undressing at bedtime in front of the mirror, checking the progress of her tan (now well down into the buttock territory). He would glance at her every once in a while over the pages of his Harold Robbins summer paperback, wanting to ask: "Are we having a problem, Charlotte, or is this merely chic despair?" But not asking. Not really wanting to know ...

Perched at the end of the long wooden dock one mid-July evening, Hershy Brahms watched the sun disappear across the lake behind a dark line of evergreens, taking with it the last hues of yellow and red from the water's surface. His feet dangled in the water which, though warm and soft to the touch, was unappetizing to the eye, having taken on a murky taupe shade near the shoreline. The dock, recently rebuilt, was redolent of fresh damp cedar. On the lawn behind him a thin cloud of smoke lifted from the outdoor charcoal grill, drifted toward the water and passed over the dock conveying the aroma of seared sirloin. Dinner was being prepared. Mushrooms simmering on the stove. Green salad. Scandinavian tablecloth and matching napkins from Bloomingdale's (imported right under the nose of an airport custom's officer who, momentarily hypnotized by Charlotte's slender suede boots, accepted Hershy's and Charlotte's false declarations without question). The meal was eaten quietly against the background of Bruckner's Eighth (Hershy's current favourite) on the stereo set.

After dinner they sat on lawn chairs, without conversation, smoking, awaiting the arrival of the Spicers, their next-door neighbours at the lake. Tootie and Larry Spicer. Tootie brought a half-platter of leftover dessert (strawberry shortcake "with real whipped cream!"); Larry bore a pitcher of homemade sangria. They talked culture. "Have you been to Stratford this season? ... Are you going to the Shaw? ... Don't you love what they're doing to Niagara-on-the-Lake! ... The Feldermans are planning to moor their yacht there for a whole week in August ... Have you ever caught Bernstein at Tanglewood? ... No? You must. It's a religious experience! ..." Down the hatch with the sangria, followed by coffee and the runny remains of the strawberry shortcake. Tootie showed off a new eighteen-carat gold chain with a gold "chai" medallion dangling just above her cleavage, given to her by Larry for their anniversary. Larry insisted on reading not one but two endless letters from their eldest son who was breaking his back for eight weeks on a kibbutz near Kiriyat Shmona. Charlotte and Hershy paid dutiful attention; they knew how meaningful these eight weeks were to Tootie and Larry. They knew also that later, when Tootie and Larry lined themselves up neatly in bed, the two of them would be entirely satisfied that their display of Show-and-Tell was just what the party needed.

In the Brahms' master bedroom the bedlamp was switched off. On arm reached over, tangled leisurely with another arm, legs entwined, Hershy squeezed against Charlotte's backside, she turned to face him and slid under as he slid over. They moved deftly, automatically. In the darkness he thought of Charlotte, imagining in his mind's eye the woman lying beneath him. His face buried in her pillow, he inhaled the natural clean scent of her hair and her perfume on the pillowcase. He thought of Tootie next door, of Fran Alter a few cottages away, of Tootie again, then travelled a half-mile south past the marina to Jenny

Felderman in the aft-cabin of the Felderman yacht. Back to Charlotte. Finished with a kaleidoscope of Charlotte-Tootie-Fran-Jenny.

Afterward, lying on his own side of the bed, Hershy wondered (as he had done increasingly of late): whom do you think of, Charlotte? In those few minutes between my first tentative caress of your shoulder and that urgent reach for Kleenex at the finale, what faces parade in and out of your consciousness; what images flash across your mental screen? Is there a Lindbergh in your life? Or an astronaunt with radar brains and airconditioned lungs? A movie star perhaps? Does some handsome black folksinger tear off his dazzling silver satin shirt and pour himself over you like oil? Is there even a Larry Spicer? Or am I really "it" – the master of the master bedroom?

Outside, a late-night breeze fanned the waters of the lake, sending them against the sandy shoreline with a steady rhythm – "whoosh ... whoosh ..." The tempo increased. The whooshing grew loud. Suddenly the waves began to pound ...

Hershy found himself clinging to the rigging near the bow of Ra I. The stern was badly warped and couldn't be hoisted above water-level, and the windward hull was hopelessly waterlogged. From a fractured yardarm, the rectangular sail hung in shreds. Splintered beyond repair, the rudder-oars dangled over the sides of the craft like broken arms. The elements – a high sea, an unrelenting wind – had conspired against Heyerdahl and Brahms and the five other men who comprised the crew. The sun, rather than look directly upon the sorry remains of this expedition, chose to hide behind heavy clouds. A rescue ship stood by, bobbing and tossing.

A decision had to be made: Abandon Ra I? Or take a desperate chance that this half-submerged basket would somehow stay afloat? They were east of Barbados, two months and three thousand nautical miles west of their starting point at Safi. Anxiously, impatiently, the crew of the rescue ship waited. Also waiting were sharks — twenty-five or thirty of the brutes — who had turned out for the occasion, in anticipation of a closing banquet.

So far the crew were evenly divided: three had voted to go on, three to abandon. Heyerdahl turned to Hershy Brahms, the seventh man. "What do you say, Brahms?" Brahms hesitated, watched the seawater cascade over the tiny craft's gunwales, counted and recounted the dark fins that appeared, disappeared and appeared again in the surrounding waves. "Abandon," he said. A trifle sardonically, one of the crew, a Russian, said: "Every ship should have at least one Jew aboard. They always choose life ..."

The seven men clambered aboard the rescue ship, leaving Ra I to spend its final hours in the company of two dozen disappointed sharks. Within minutes, aboard the rescue ship, Heyerdahl and his mates were planning the construction of a new craft — Ra II — and comparing notes of mistakes to be avoided next time out. There would certainly be a next time out, no doubt about that. Within months the twin keels of the new craft would attach themselves to the surface of the Atlantic, cling stubbornly to every wavecrest, seeking that magic current just off the Canary Islands that would draw it westward, westward ...

In the stillness of the cottage bedroom Hershy Brahms could hear another summer limping past him. Summer, for Brahms, had always begun with maximum expectations; summer was a time when the world came out of storage, a time when something new, exciting, challenging might break for him: ("Mr. Brahms, the Premier and Cabinet have decided you're just the man to head ..."). And though by mid-August every year he realized that autumn would arrive all too quickly and be followed by winter, and life would simply go on as it had always gone on, he was never quite pre-

69

pared for that final foreclosure of his summery hopes, never quite ready to face the repetition of last year's names and faces and numbers.

Before long, Hershy told himself, Thor Heyerdahl would once again be searching the night sky over the South Atlantic and, pinpointing his star, would follow it.

And where would Hershy Brahms be searching? Would he, like Lenny Winston, spend the rest of his nights probing the thicket between his legs and, locating his star, his ever-ready ever-ascending star, follow it?

That wasn't enough, Brahms told himself. There had to be more. Remember what the Russian said: "... They always choose life ..."

Yes, of course Hershy Brahms chose life. That choice was in his blood, as basic as corpuscles.

Therefore, there had to be more.

The pair of tickets arrived in the morning mail — one pink for Rosh Hashonah, the other blue for Yom Kippur, both inscribed "Mr. and Mrs. Hershel Brahms and Kevin." On each ticket, just below the names, in bold type, this note of stern prohibition: "Not transferable." Hershy watched out of the corners of his eyes as Charlotte tacked them to the kitchen bulletin board. His face bore an expression of deep gloom. For Hershy Brahms, the arrival every year, in late August, of tickets for the High Holy Days was like the falling of the first dead leaves from the poplars and maples in the countryside. Two innocuous rectangles of cardboard, yet somehow they smothered the hopes of June and July and spread splotches of rust over the diminishing patch of green that Brahms clung to as the days shortened and the evening air sharpened.

Therefore, the gloom.

Charlotte had posted the tickets prominently alongside the police and fire department emergency numbers and next to an overdue property tax bill.

"This will never do," Hershy said, sliding out of the breakfast nook. He crossed to the bulletin board, removed the tickets and fixed them with a magnetic clip to the front of the refrigerator.

"Why did you do that?" Charlotte asked.

"Because I'm a firm believer in the separation of Church and State."

"I don't think it's anything to joke about," she said. "I want you to come with me and Kevin this year."

"Forget it."

"Please!"

Hershy gulped down his glass of orange juice. "Thanks for breakfast. I'll have my coffee at the office."

"Hershy," Charlotte said, "please don't run away every time this subject comes up."

"Who's running away?"

"You are."

"Okay. Drop the subject and I'll stay for an onion roll."

"I can't drop the subject – not this year, anyway. This year it's different."

"Wherefore is this year different from all other years? Aren't there still two sittings – the early show and the late show? Or are they toying with the idea of going into overtime?"

"You don't fool me, Hershy," Charlotte said. "Your little wisecracks are just a cover-up. The fact is you feel guilty and ashamed that you never bothered to attend services."

The fact was that for years, on Rosh Hashonah and Yom Kippur, Hershy and Louis Brahms chose to worship at Woodbine Race Track. Even when it rained.

Hershy remembered the old days in the little synagogue near Dundas Street:

His father always sat in the rearmost pew, reading a copy of *The Forward* that was folded neatly to fit within the covers of the prayer book, totally absorbed in the obituary of a Galician-born department store owner from Schenectady whose two sons and one daughter

71

were all physicians. "Fucking Galizianer," Louis would mutter. "They have all the luck." Near the heavily varnished altar at the front of the room, a rabbi, looking as if he had just hit town after forty years on the desert, stood mumbling incoherently in Hebrew, bowing and bending and beating the caved-in portion of his upper torso that had once been a chest. It was Yom Kippur, the end of one religious-fiscal year, the beginning of another – a time to look back on sins past and look forward to sins future. Time to make a deal with God, to get off the hook with Him for wild promises you made that couldn't be honoured if you stood on your head. Time also to settle certain contractual and moral disputes with your fellow man. Well, not so fast ... maybe. Maybe today, tomorrow, sometime later this year. Or maybe never.

Hershy remembered Louis' swollen wallet containing the unbanked proceeds of yesterday's business, unbanked because it didn't look good if the goyim saw you in their banks on the holiest of holy days. He could still detect in his nostrils the smell emanating from the fish market that was separated from the synagogue by a narrow litter-strewn alley, and the halitosis of repentance everywhere in the still air around him. Late in the day Louis would slip quietly out of the packed room, deposit the Jewish newspaper in the Chrysler parked discreetly a block away and slip back in for the final blast of the shofar signalling the end of the Day of Atonement.

A few moments later Louis would be standing at the sweet-table in the synagogue basement, balancing in his left hand a small tumbler of Crown Royal (God only knew where the sexton found Crown Royal during World War II) and a piece of honey cake, shaking the hand of and wishing a happy new year to a man he positively loathed. The man would grin and peel away the lapel of Louis' suit-jacket, and point to a fountain pen protruding from Louis' vest pocket. "Thou shalt not carry a fountain pen nor any other writing instrument on this Day," the peeler would say, still grinning. Calling the man a son-of-a-bitch for the sin of not minding his own business on this holiest of holy days, Louis would swallow the piece of honey cake in a single bite and pull at Hershy's arm. "C'mon Hersheleh, let's get the hell out of here before I choke."

That was Yom Kippur, 1944. There were just two or three more Yom Kippurs at the old synagogue. Then Louis decided it was time to look for God in other places. Woodbine, with its green fields, its view of Lake Ontario, and the passing brownish blur of horseflesh, seemed as likely a place as any to find Him.

For Charlotte Brahms there were memories that came from the other – the right – side of the religious tracks; candied memories that were pleasant to taste and retaste and that sweetened with age.

As a kindergarten child she had sat correctly upright in the vast main sanctuary gaping at the torahs that stood like tall bejewelled wedding cakes within the open arc on the dais, sat secure between her father's after-shave cologne on one side and her mother's powdery rosy smell on the other. At centre stage stood the rabbi, blackrobed, his outstretched arms resembling wings, a benign hawk blessing a field of attentive sparrows.

As a teenager she had worn an ankle-length white dress and black robe at her class confirmation and barely held back tears during the confirmation pledge ("Ever faithful we shall be ..."); had memorized the hymns that all sounded as if they'd been composed by Beethoven or Haydn for some solemn Germanic rite (at thirty-seven she still sang along quietly with the choir, for this was the very temple to which the Hershel Brahmses now belonged). She and Hershy had been married there. Kevin had been named in that same cool spacious sanctuary. She loved the architectural symmetry, the Romanesque arches, the vivid jigsaws of stained glass depicting Abraham and Rebecca and the downfall of evil tyrants and the gathering of bountiful harvests. She loved the sculptures and reflecting pool in the inner courtyard and the distinguished-looking silver haired men dressed in ambassadorial morning suits who ushered her to her seat on Saturday mornings.

More than twenty years had passed since the heart-tug of Confirmation Day and yet, each time she came within the beige and oak confines of that temple, she was once again young Charlotte Zimmerman, fresh-faced but with the faintest touch of rouge on her cheeks, virginal, the good daughter, the diligent doer of her homework and passer of grades, the conscientious summer camp counsellor, awaiting the inevitable call to Jewish wifehood and motherhood; accepting, always accepting, bowing her head and shutting her eyes tightly during prayers, and not the least embarrassed to let her voice project over the voices of other worshippers during responsive readings.

Hershy looked at his watch. "My God, time to scoot downtown and climb up into my little cage," he said, pretending to be bravely cheerful. Then, perceiving that his wife looked strangely narrow-shouldered and lonely standing in her flannel nightgown in the middle of the kitchen, and knowing he had frustrated her (and feeling a twinge of guilt) he added: "You still haven't told me what's so important about this year."

"It's Kevin's bar mitzvah year. He starts his lessons in a couple of weeks."

"So — who's stopping him?"

"For Godsake Hershy, it's not a question of who's stopping him. It's a question of who's encouraging him. I do all I can, but you and ..."

"Me and who? Go on Charlotte, tell me, me and who?"

"You and Lou." Charlotte hesitated.

"Leave Lou out of this, Charlotte. My father may not be the nice pious old man you dreamed of having as Kevin's grandfather, but he and the kid are crazy about each other."

"That's not enough for a boy Kevin's age."

"It's more than enough as far as I'm concerned. Just leave Lou out of this."

"All right, we'll leave Lou out, like you say." Charlotte's voice wavered; she was fighting to control herself. "But that doesn't settle the matter of your responsibility. You owe it to your son to make the effort."

"I don't want to get involved with that place, Charlotte. How many times must I tell you!"

"Just this once Hershy, for Kevin's sake."

"I can't."

"But why? *Why?*"

"Charlotte, I've told you God-knows-how-many times, the idea of parking myself inside three million dollars worth of real estate and praying for miracles is poison to me. I feel closer to God at the roof bar of the Park Plaza."

"All I ask, Hershy, is that you make an exception just this one time ... for Kevin's sake."

Hershy studied Charlotte for a moment. Then quietly, as if caressing a witness into an admission of guilt, he said: "Come on now Charlotte, that's not quite honest, is it?"

"What's not quite honest?"

"That 'for Kevin's sake' routine. It's Rachel Mannheim you're worried about, isn't it? How'll it look to Big Sister if Charlotte Brahms comes down the aisle without hubby suitably in tow? That's what's really eating you, isn't it?"

"Rachel Mannheim has nothing to do with this, nothing at all ..." Charlotte's voice trailed off feebly. She knew, and Hershy knew, that it was otherwise.

Rachel Mannheim – Big Sister as Hershy liked to call her – had become a major presence in the life of Charlotte Brahms.

Earlier in the year Mrs. Mannheim had won election to the presidency of the temple, the first woman to hold that office since the congregation was organized at the turn of the century. That her victory was historic was beyond argument. That it heralded the beginning of happy times for the temple congregation and staff was, however, a matter of heated debate.

Optimists counted on Mrs. Mannheim to demonstrate that she could accomplish at least as much in a single year as her male predecessors had accomplished in seventy. Heartened by her unquenchable ambition and energy, they predicted an era of reform, and when she vowed in her acceptance speech "to reduce the red tape to God and the high cost of worship," they smiled with quiet satisfaction and sat back to enjoy the spectacle of heads rolling.

Pessimists dreaded the very qualities that endeared Mrs. Mannheim to the optimists, and warned that in her zeal she would commit all sorts of reckless and excessive acts. Her desire for power and her outspoken determination gave sleepless nights to this group, many of whom over the years had grown sedentary and paunchy in the temple's service. They regarded the prospect of Mrs. Mannheim's crusades with little or no enthusiasm.

Charlotte Brahms was one of the optimists. Indeed she was more than that, for her signature was one of the five on Rachel Mannheim's nomination. She had campaigned vigorously for Mrs. Mannheim's election, spending hours on the telephone and even writing urgent personal letters to boost her candidate's cause. So fervently did Charlotte labour that it seemed to Hershy that female suffrage itself, and not merely a Mannheim victory, was at stake.

Being neither optimist nor pessimist, but a dedicated neutral, Hershy looked upon all this fuss as if it were a minor earth tremor in Siberia. At Charlotte's urging, he had cast a vote for Rachel Mannheim, figuring "What the hell." But when Charlotte sought to enlist his participation on the temple legal committee, Hershy Brahms laid down an impossible condition: "I'll serve, but only if Rachel Mannheim agrees to appoint me a Queen's Counsel in her New Year's Honours List." And that was the end of that.

In keeping with what Mrs. Mannheim regarded as her executive style, "The President's Corner" in the weekly temple bulletin was shifted from page three to page one and renamed "Levelling With The Pres." The substance of the column also changed; where her predecessors had seen fit to serve up oven-warm batches of platitudes every week, Mrs. Mannheim poked her editorial broom into corners that hadn't felt the touch of a bristle in years. In addition, presidential memos that began "In the interest of economy and efficiency . . ." descended like messages of doom upon the office staff (who secretly nicknamed Mrs. Mann-heim "President Paperclip"). The cantor, the principal of the religious school, the librarian – once all virtu-ally unimpeachable – found themselves fidgeting ner-vously like errant schoolboys on the presidential carpet every time some transgression was committed within their respective bailiwicks.

No one, it seemed, could find shelter from the new president's penetrating scrutiny. Some said that before too many months passed God would find that even He was not above being summoned to the president's office if things went wrong in her temple.

All these transitions Charlotte Brahms viewed with wholehearted approval. "It reminds me of John Ken-nedy's First Hundred Days," she glowed.

"You mean Genghis Khan's, don't you?" said Hershy.

Everyone was occupied exchanging choice pieces of hearsay. At the focal point of the gossip stood the two rabbis. It was no secret that several years earlier, when their contracts had come up for renewal, Mrs. Mann-heim had fought against the generous salary raises awarded to them, pointing out that they were already earning more than many of their colleagues in the rabbinate, and that their standards of living were downright palatial compared with the austerity and self-denial of some of their Christian counterparts. The rabbis in turn pointed out that the temple was one of the major Jewish institutions in the city – indeed in the whole country – and it was reasonable that their salaries should be commensurate with that fact.

It was also no secret that, economics aside, she had long considered both clergymen guilty of certain operational sins. For one thing, she charged, they had managed to divide their duties into convenient zones, the senior rabbi concentrating his attentions upon the older congregants, the junior rabbi upon the younger, thus leaving a large population of the middle-aged with seemingly no other function at the temple than to sell raffle tickets. For another – and this she regarded as the more serious charge – they had escalated their involvement with "social protest" issues to the point where their purely rabbinical roles had become secondary to what she termed "sidewalk activism."

By a coincidence of timing, the two contracts were due for reconsideration early in Mrs. Mannheim's term, and the word was out that one rabbi – or both rabbis for that matter – might become expendable.

The senior rabbi, Emanuel Shulman, was in his late fifties. Despite a touch of arthritis, he played an agressive game of tennis, was almost as effective at golf, and for the past five years was the champion runner in his age group at the Jewish Y. The same vigour that permeated his athletic endeavours carried over into his sermons which, despite their biblical allusions and intellectual junkets, often sounded rather like pre-game pep talks. He was a spiritual cheerleader; one hospital visit from Rabbi Shulman, it was said, was a better cure than all the doctors, medical machinery and pills put together. At parties he was a witty raconteur, the star of any circle in which he found himself.

By contrast, Howard Roher, the junior of the two, was rather shy. He preferred small groups to large gatherings and shunned centre stage unless duty called him to it. Above all, he avoided physical exercise as if it were a social disease. Unlike Shulman, Roher was a bachelor. This left him free during off-hours to devote himself to his two passions – the cinema, and a dark green Alfa Romeo sports coupe (dark green being more conservative, as befitted a rabbi). Younger congregants (a few of whom were privileged, off limits, to call him Howard) delighted in arguing with him about the relative virtues of Truffaut and Fellini, and nodded knowledgeably when the young rabbi quoted Dylan and Kerouac in his sermons.

Both clergymen stationed themselves regularly at the forefront of the public conscience, parading beanth placards that denounced the war in Vietnam, international terrorism and the proliferation of nuclear arms. Like somberly-clad pied pipers they often led the Temple's teenagers in public demonstrations against one sort of iniquity or another. After one such demonstration Kevin Brahms returned home much later than expected.

"Well, revolutionary," Hershy called out as Kevin sank exhausted into a down-filled sofa, "what social injustice did you attack today?"

"Migrant workers in California."

"What! You attacked migrant workers?"

"Gawd, Dad. I mean the exploitation of migrant workers," Kevin said, disgusted that his father should be so thickheaded.

"Uh huh, I knew it!" Hershy said, feigning extreme upset. "We'll be blacklisted by every supermarket in town. I'll never see a grapefruit again."

"What took you so long, Kevin?" Charlotte asked. "I thought the rally would be over by five."

"It was, but Shulman and Roher made us hang around Nathan Phillips Square for an hour. I think they were looking for a chance to disturb the peace."

Each rabbi was deeply conscious of his own strengths and weaknesses. Shulman sensed that the young regarded his views as rather Kiplingesque and corny. He wished for the kind of easy rapport with them that Roher so obviously enjoyed. On the other hand, whenever Roher officiated at an assembly of older congregants he felt as if he were standing before them in knee pants, and wished he could take on overnight the aura of elder statesman that Shulman had acquired during twenty years in the pulpit.

Though the two men turned their eyes heavenward as duty required, they kept their ears to the ground from whence came unmistakeable rumblings of crisis. Each began to look upon the other as a possible rival. Questions gnawed: "Will I be the one to survive? And if not, where will I go?"

With contract renewals and questions of salary looming, and Rachel Mannheim's gavel poised like an axe, what were they to do? Both rabbis, reasoning matters over, concluded that in union there might not only be comfort but immunity from dismissal. But neither told the other. Not in the beginning, at least. Throughout the first four or five months of the Mannheim regime, they kept their private thoughts tightly bottled up.

It was on the eve of their preliminary contract talks with Mrs. Mannheim that the first spills occurred.

Rabbi Roher was preparing to conduct a late afternoon service in the small chapel and attempting, without success, to switch on the electric candelabra on the lectern.

"Bloody — !" Roher whispered, forgetting that the acoustics in the small chapel could magnify even a slight hiccup into a nationwide broadcast. Shulman, who happened to be passing the chapel doorway, popped his head in.

"Trouble?"

Roher pointed in disgust to the candelabra. "Doesn't work. Must be a short somewhere. I'm adding that to my list too."

Shulman came into the chapel. "What list?"

"I'm sending a list to Ralph Nader — all the things around here that don't work."

"Oh," said Shulman, amused by his colleague's obvious disgruntlement. "Such as?"

"Such as this stupid candelabra."

"One complaint doesn't make a list."

"I've got lots more," Roher said. "The P.A. system's on the fritz again; the new torah doesn't unwind properly —"

"Maybe it's prophetic in some way," Rabbi Shulman said. "Maybe all these annoyances are meant to be – especially the thing with the torah. Have you considered that?"

"I'm a practical man, not a philosopher," Roher said. "Things don't work, I just drop a line to Ralph Nader. I believe in action."

"By the way," Shulman said, whispering, "you won't forget to switch off the chapel lights when you're finished, will you? Remember, Howard, our electric bill is up thirteen percent this year."

Roher corrected him: "Fourteen percent. That is, according to Mrs. Mannheim's latest memo on the subject in the Bulletin." Roher wagged a warning finger at Shulman. "Obviously you haven't been reading 'Levelling With The Pres.' faithfully."

"On the contrary, Rabbi," Shulman retorted with the same mock severity, "not only do I read 'Levelling With The Pres.' faithfully, I read it religiously! What more can a rabbi do?"

"Pray, brother, pray."

Something in Roher's countenance as he said this told Shulman that these few moments of levity were over. "I gather, Howard, you received the same 'engraved' invitation to meet with our president that I received?"

"Yes. This morning."

"Like Fate knocking at the door, wasn't it?"

"Yes."

Shulman studied his colleague, then very gingerly he asked: "Tell me, what do you think of Rachel Mannheim?"

"Frankly?"

"Frankly."

"We're speaking confidentially?"

"Of course," Shulman said.

"Okay," said Roher, "frankly and confidentially, she scares the living hell out of me."

Shulman nodded in solemn agreement. "Among other qualities," he said, "it's that pale flawless complexion, and those silver-gray eyes of hers."

"I swear," Roher said, "looking into those eyes is like staring into an empty refrigerator."

For a moment, the two rabbis stood hushed in the dim light of the small chapel, thinking about Mrs. Mannheim, and shivering in unison. Ever mindful of the acoustics, Shulman said very softly: "Howard, when you write Mr. Nader, ask if it's possible to get Rachel Mannheim recalled."

It was no surprise to Rabbis Shulman and Roher that their preliminary talks with the president went poorly. Grudgingly, Mrs. Mannheim agreed that length of service – twenty years in Shulman's case, six in Roher's – was an element to be considered. She was even willing to concede that the rabbis were diligent in fulfilling certain practical roles in the clubs for senior congregants, for teenagers, the young marrieds' counselling service, the sick visitation service, as well as in their participation in Israel bond drives and United Jewish Appeal campaigns. "Mind you," she added, "there are those among us who question your involvement with the current Vietnam issue ... who feel that the anti-war movement is essentially political."

"On the contrary," Shulman objected, "it is essentially a matter of conscience, and therefore concerns us directly."

"Come now," she said, smiling condescendingly, "do you really believe that the war will be ended by clergymen on Toronto's street corners shouting for it to stop? The fact is, gentlemen, that the war will be settled by hard-nosed diplomats making deals at peace tables."

"In other words, Madam President, you're telling us public outcry has no significance?"

"No. I'm simply saying that your contracts do not call for you to join in such public outcry as if it were a part of this temple's tradition."

"With the greatest respect," said Shulman, "a synagogue does not exist in a vacuum. Traditionally, it is the centre of all Jewish community life, not merely religious activity. And a rabbi is not simply a floor-walker in a religious department store."

"What you call 'practical roles,' Mrs. Mannheim," Roher added, "are in many cases indistinguishable from spiritual roles. The lowly application of a Band-Aid to a cut finger carries with it a kind of faith, an unspoken affirmation of life. Often it can be as important a lesson as an hour's lecture about some homily in the Midrash."

"That's a charming concept, I'm sure," the president said. "But we have physicians to dispense Band-Aids. From our rabbis we expect teaching, scholarship of a very high level, and, of course, religious inspiration."

"My dear lady," Shulman said, "I can't envision a single religious function that doesn't contain non-religious ingredients."

"Which explains, I suppose, movie reviews in the temple bulletin?" she said coolly.

Shulman reddened. "That's not quite fair, Mrs. Mannheim. Rabbi Roher's recent reviews of *The Graduate* and *Rosemary's Baby* were totally appropriate. Both had to do with sacrificing one's soul for one kind of devil or another."

"Perhaps. I'm afraid I haven't had time to see those two films – or any films in recent months for that matter. How I envy your moments of leisure."

"Even moments of leisure can be productive," said Roher.

"That depends on whether or not such productivity is relevant."

"Relevant to what?"

"To the synagogue."

"Madam President," Shulman interjected, "the question today is not whether the world around us is relevant to the synagogue, but whether the synagogue still has any relevance to the world. It makes no difference that the subject is a kid out of college who can't find a place for himself in modern society, or a whole nation that has misjudged its place on this planet. These matters, and all shades in between, concern us vitally."

"They may be matters of concern, but, if you'll pardon my bluntness, the depth of your concern is out of proportion. A rabbi's primary field of competence is supposed to be Torah. Relevance, as you seem to employ the word, isn't everything."

"Surely the proof that we're succeeding is in the audiences," Shulman suggested. "Our sanctuary has never been fuller."

"Yes, but look who makes up your audiences: the older folk, who come out of habit and often out of fear – fear that they are getting close to the end. And young people, yes, they too show up, many out of compulsion, or because some long-haired flowerchild is going to play the guitar and sing chic little songs about freedom for the American Indian."

"I find that dreadfully cynical."

"Cynical or not, Rabbi Shulman, according to a report I've commissioned on membership retention, your audiences comprise fewer and fewer middle-aged congregants. Frankly, they are turned off by all this social-action fretting."

"We had no idea," Shulman said, "that a report was being prepared. My colleague and I might have wanted to make our own contributions to such a report."

"I take responsibility for that decision," said Mrs. Mannheim. "I thought it best to approach the subject as objectively as possible."

"And who, may we ask, did the job ... objectively, that is?"

Ignoring Shulman's sarcasm, Rachel Mannheim replied: "Who performed the special assignment is unimportant." Despite the rabbis' patent irritation, Mrs. Mannheim saw no reason to disclose that the author of the report was Charlotte Brahms. Why expose a staunch and trusted ally to what could turn out to be a hurricane of rabbinical wrath?

Shulman continued to press. "But we should at least have some opportunity to challenge such findings."

"I tell you, gentlemen," Mrs. Mannheim persisted, "that there is an important segment who are not getting what they want."

"And just what is it that they want?"

"They want, and indeed they deserve, a little peace of mind when they leave the temple."

"A moment ago," Roher pointed out, "you told us relevance isn't everything. Neither is peace of mind . . ."

On the matter of salaries Rachel Mannheim came to the point promptly and without sidestepping a fraction of an inch. "I cannot, in all good conscience, recommend to the board anything more than a nominal increase based on the cost-of-living index." Times were difficult. Inflation made no exception in the case of a synagogue. Besides, she insisted, it was a demonstrated fact that expenditures and spirituality always moved inversely; when one rose, the other automatically fell.

Nothing was resolved. Politely, but curtly, the adversaries said their goodbyes.

In the corridor outside the board room, Shulman said: "Now I know how Shigemitsu must have felt that day on the deck of the Missouri."

From Roher there issued a long drawn-out sigh of dejection. "After six years," he said, "it's finally dawned on me what that old expression really means."

"What old expression?"

"Graying at the temples."

Sunday nights and cold leftovers — a combination that never failed to get Hershy Brahms down. Ever since his childhood he had loathed Sunday nights (because invariably they led to Monday mornings) and cold leftovers (because invariably they tasted like wax paper or, in more recent years, tinfoil). Charlotte, noting how her husband poked a disinterested fork into the remains of the previous Friday night's roast, gently pushed a bottle of H.P. Sauce in his direction. "Put some of that on it," she suggested.

"Charlotte, if I were dying you'd offer me H.P. Sauce. Can't you understand," Hershy became melodramatic, clutching his forehead in an imitation of Peter Lorre, "I need a hot meal – you remember, the kind you have to blow on. Even Cream of Wheat!"

"Tomorrow night for sure," Charlotte promised. "I just didn't have time today."

"Another marathon session at Rachel Mannheim's?"

"Yes."

Eagerly Hershy asked: "Did she serve anything hot?"

"Only tea. Mind you, there was an awfully appetizing smell coming from Rachel's kitchen."

"She was probably cooking somebody's goose." As he said this, Hershy attempted an ominous expression but it was no use; he couldn't for the life of him disguise his amusement over the case of Mannheim versus Shulman and Roher. It struck him as supreme comic irony that the spiritual leaders of the temple were paid to pray as part of the daily ritual for the shedding of divine light upon the president of the congregation, while she – the intended beneficiary of these supplications – thought only in terms of chopping off their heads.

It wasn't especially difficult for Hershy Brahms to stay put on the outer fringes of this trouble. After all, the three principals were thus far no more than bit players on the stage of his life.

His last contact with Rabbi Shulman occurred years earlier when they were paired against each other in a tournament at the tennis club. "Hi," Hershy had said, extending his hand across the net, "I'm Hershel

Brahms, but you can call me Hershy." "Hi," Shulman returned, "I'm Rabbi Shulman, but you can call me Rabbi." Having lost the opening round, Hershy went on to lose the rally for service and eventually the set itself. "It's hopeless," Hershy confided later to Lenny Winston in the locker room, referring to Shulman. "I can't pray with him, and I'll be damned if I'll *play* with him."

His one and only experience with Roher took place following a lecture the young rabbi had delivered on the work of Edward Albee. It was shortly after *Who's Afraid of Virginia Woolf* became the dramatic darling of the temple literati and Charlotte had twisted Hershy's arm to attend. In Roher's generous view the Albee play represented the most important advance in the theatre since the introduction of folding seats. Lining up for coffee in the auditorium Hershy unexpectedly found himself face to face with Roher. Not certain what to say, Brahms uttered the first thing that came into his mind: "I enjoyed your lecture, Rabbi; but I'll be interested to hear what you think about ten years hence." Without batting an eye, Roher quipped: " 'Ten Years Hence?' Haven't heard of it. Is it a new play?" All the way home Hershy Brahms lectured himself: "That'll teach you to fuck around with Gene Autry." He felt like a wounded Apache.

As for Rachel Mannheim, Hershy Brahms could never quite understand the nature of the woman's appeal. What others chose to regard as charisma, Hershy looked upon as a carefully crafted persona, an impressive – even stunning – public facade which, as she stood before her full-length mirror in her dressingroom, fragmented into a set of studied poses, rehearsed gestures, cleverly spoken catch-phrases. Hershy imagined Rachel Mannheim's closet crammed with hundreds of hangers, each bearing not only the right costume for the right occasion but the appropriate face to go with it; each face discreetly tagged "Synthetic Material – Dry Clean Only."

Far better, Hershy Brahms admonished himself, to maintain a firmly fixed distance at all times between himself and these people.

And yet (though he wouldn't for a moment admit this to anyone, including Charlotte) he was beginning to feel occasional twinges of sympathy for Shulman and Roher.

As a lawyer he understood the peculiar advantages and disadvantages in a life devoted to selling professional services. To Hershy it seemed comparatively easy, and often so attractive, to earn one's living in commodities that could be sold by the foot or the dozen or the pound; tangibles that could be wrapped and passed across the counter in exchange for immediate payment. The vending of professional services, on the other hand, was such a nebulous business. Who could really weigh intelligence? measure experience? package skill?

Especially difficult was it for a rabbi, Hershy thought. Doctors, lawyers, sociologists, economists – all these so-called experts at least enjoyed the comforts and security of their specialized vocabularies. Confronted by the inexplicable, a lawyer could dazzle his client with a string of "whereases" and "hereinafters;" a physician could attach a Latin label to his diagnosis and thus strike awe in the mind of his patient; the economist or the sociologist could always fall back upon his favourite trick – hyphenating long words into portentous phrases. In these professions, Jargon equalled Mystique – that was the unfailing equation of power. The average layman could do nothing more than press his nose against the outer windowpane, peering in, pretending to understand.

By comparison, rabbis, in Hershy's view, stood before their flocks naked, with few tools available to them to deal with the inexplicable other than the force of their egos and a handbook or two of simplistic verses and old-fashioned scriptures. All the scholarly tracts and treatises on their shelves were precious little help in explaining the strange and terrible destinies that regu-

88

larly befall mankind. No act was tougher to follow than an Act of God. And yet a rabbi was expected to do precisely that. Envy the life of a rabbi? Never!

Still, the twinges Hershy felt of late were not sharp enough to compel him to become a partisan. Not yet, at any rate. Life was too short to dissipate one's energies in the arena of synagogue politics. Besides, the Brahms family had already made its contribution in that arena: Charlotte, being a member of Mrs. Mannheim's inner circle, was on call at all hours of the day or night and seemed to thrive on the atmosphere of urgency that infused everything at the temple.

"Tell me something, Charlotte," Hershy said setting aside a half-eaten coldplate, "is there any truth to these rumours that somebody has done a double hatchet job on Shulman and Roher?"

"I don't know what you're referring to."

"All this buzzing about some confidential membership retention report Mannheim's been waving in their faces. Apparently she won't let them examine it, and she insists that the hatchet man – or hatchet woman – remain anonymous."

"I don't know too much about it."

"C'mon Charlotte, you must know. Christ, you're closer to Rachel Mannheim than her girdle."

"Why are you suddenly so interested, Hershy?"

"I'm not. It just offends my sense of justice to think that anybody in this day and age would pull a stunt like that in a religious institution. Hell, it smacks of inquisitions and burnings and the rack."

Charlotte smiled sweetly. "Suppose, my darling champion of the overdog, I were to tell you *I* wrote that report."

Hershy studied Charlotte's expression. In her smile he noted a hint of roguish mischief. Could she be serious? Could she? He threw back his head and laughed. "Bullshit!"

"You don't believe me?"

"Bull*shit*," Hershy said, still laughing. Then looking at his wife, he said: "I love when you try to tell a lie, Charlotte. You are so charmingly inept at it."

"Thank you for the compliment," Charlotte said. "Tomorrow night I'll make you a hot meal ... the kind you have to blow on."

A special meeting of the board was called. One item only appeared on the agenda: the matter of the rabbis' contracts. Like all meetings under Rachel Mannheim's chairmanship, it began on time; not a soul was late, not a pencil or sheet of paper out of place on the long boardroom table.

Mrs. Mannheim, speaking from notes penned in her own flawless hand, delivered a full account of her talk with Shulman and Roher. Her tone was dispassionate, her exhibition of fairness nothing less than exquisite. She hoped – indeed expected – that the very act on her part of not tipping the scales would win immediate and broad support for her stand.

To her surprise she encountered vigorous opposition. The instant she closed her mouth and put down her notes, fires broke out along the perimeter of the table.

"These men are spiritual leaders – not hired hands!"

"But leadership implies service. Rabbis exist to serve the temple, not vice versa."

"Servants or not, they can't live on psalms."

"Don't worry about Shulman's diet, he's been living well off this temple for twenty years. Next thing you know he'll be insisting his job's guaranteed for life, like a wristwatch."

"You can't just dump a man who's poured some of the best years of his life into this congregation."

"Roher has only poured six."

"Six or twenty, the principle's the same."

"Too bad but that's the way the rabbinical cookie crumbles."

In the midst of the din one thin raspy voice called for the floor. "Please, madam chairman, please, may I say something ..." Rachel Mannheim's gavel cracked like riflefire. "The chair recognizes Mr. Cooperman."

J. Samuel Cooperman, a retired lawyer, was the oldest director on the temple board, eighty-three years of age, with the appearance of a sun-dried iguana. He rose unsteadily. In his hand, which shook with the first signs of Parkinson's Disease, he held copies of both Shulman's and Roher's employment contracts. "I think we are overlooking a crucial fact in each of these agreements . . ."

Everyone suddenly fell silent. Whenever old Sam Cooperman came across a point everyone else had overlooked, it usually meant the sky was about to fall.

"These agreements follow a precedent that's been in use at this temple ever since I first became a director over forty years ago. Each provides that if, after five years' service or more, a rabbi's employment is not about to be renewed, he must be given a full twelve months' advance notice before the expiration of the then current term of his contract."

"Otherwise?" Mrs. Mannheim asked.

"Otherwise," Cooperman rasped, "his employment is deemed to have been automatically renewed for the same term of years, in which event, if his salary cannot be mutually agreed upon, the matter must be submitted to arbitration."

All eyes turned now to the president. Making a prodigious effort to maintain her composure, she asked: "Mr. Cooperman, are you telling us that we have gone past our deadline . . . that the contracts are now deemed to be renewed?"

"Exactly."

"Are you also saying that we are now obliged to negotiate?"

"I am."

The room was hushed now.

Someone half-whispered: "Who the devil ever invented those contracts?"

"I did," Cooperman answered, matter-of-factly. Then he sat down.

Another pause. Rachel Mannheim leaned forward in her armchair, back straight, head held high, every inch an empress surveying her courtiers before dismissing them. "This matter clearly requires further study. I'm therefore going to call for a motion to adjourn the meeting for one week."

Before she could finish, there were indignant shouts of "No! ... no adjournment! ... let's get on with it now! ..." But the Mannheim forces were sufficient to carry the motion to adjourn – though barely.

By weekend all channels of synagogue gossip strained under an overload of rumours. Two rumours took priority. The first was that Rachel Mannheim had conferred privately with Derek Hollenberg, the resident genius of McCarthy, Blake and Fraser, to determine the possibility of undoing that which – if one accepted Cooperman's interpretation – seemed to have been so irrevocably done. The second rumour had it that the faction opposed to the president was closing ranks in preparation for mutiny, and had retained as its legal advisor Gordon Clarkson, a specialist in constitutional issues (who was bound to be absolutely untainted, being of Scottish descent).

One week later, in an atmosphere of hostility and mistrust, the board of directors resumed its deliberations.

It turned out that both rumours were true.

Rachel Mannheim had indeed conferred with Hollenberg. In her most imperial voice she read aloud his letter of opinion: "... Faced with the vague and archaic terminology of these agreements, I express grave doubts," Hollenberg wrote, "as to the employees' ability to enforce the 'automatic renewal' provisions should they decline to accept what they might regard as an unsatisfactory salary judgment of the arbitration committee ... on the other hand, the employer's rights are somewhat clouded as well by reason of the same terminology ..."

As she continued to read Hollenberg's opinion, interruptions came rudely from all sides. Again and again

Mrs. Mannheim rapped her gavel, demanding order, but the acrimonious exchanges only persisted and grew in volume.

Hollenberg's letter concluded: "I respectfully take the liberty of observing that a realistic and thorough revision of the temple's employee contracts, at rabbinical level, is probably long overdue."

At these words, J. Samuel Cooperman began opening and shutting his mouth in rapid succession. The old iguana seemed to be snapping at invisible flies – the only physical means available to him to demonstrate his anger. Finally he managed to get to his feet and squeak: "Damned impertinence!"

A bit defensively, Mrs. Mannheim said: "I consider Mr. Hollenberg's letter extremely erudite."

"Extremely adipose is more like it," ventured one of her opponents.

Another added: "It was more like a speech from the throne."

Mrs. Mannheim blazed. "That remark is both tasteless and entirely out of order!"

At this point the other principal rumour came alive: with uncanny timing, Mrs. Mannheim's opposition rose as one and, without so much as a word of excuse or explanation, trooped briskly out of the boardroom.

Alone, at a corner of the table remote from the president, sat Sam Cooperman, a solitary lizard in a suddenly-defoliated jungle, still snapping grumpily at invisible flies. At last he too cranked himself up out of his seat, nodded curtly in Mrs. Mannheim's direction, and shuffled foot by foot out of the room. "Well," murmured the recording secretary, "there goes our quorum."

The meeting was over.

Sound travels faster than the speed of light whenever bad news is being transmitted from the innards of a synagogue. Accordingly, the latest uproar in the boardroom reached the ears of the entire congregation in record time.

Then, with equal speed, the uproar went public.

Encouraged by Gordon Clarkson, the anti-Mannheimers took a full page in the *Canadian Jewish Times* to denounce "the crude undermining by the president of all the humanitarian principles" for which the temple had stood, and to declare their support for the rabbis.

With the publication of this proclamation of war, the pressures upon the rabbis began driving them into separate states of torment.

Rabbi Shulman's arthritis troubled him more than usual, and he couldn't bring himself to go near a tennis court or a gymnasium. During his hospital visits it was sometimes difficult to distinguish between patient and visitor, so morose was he much of the time.

As for Rabbi Roher, in a moment of extreme preoccupation with the current upheaval, he failed to brake properly in a line of rush-hour traffic, and his beloved Alfa Romeo ended up being carted off the rain-soaked street like a dead horse.

The accident gave Shulman an excuse to pay a sympathy visit to his colleague.

"Sorry to hear about your car," Shulman said. "Another case for Ralph Nader?"

"Nope," replied Roher lugubriously. "I did it all myself. The memorial service is tomorrow."

"Memorial service?"

"For the Alfa ... they tell me it's a total writeoff. Shiva will be in my apartment. In lieu of flowers, please donate to The Ontario Motor League."

Shulman managed a wan smile. "I believe the customary quotation is: 'These are the times that try men's souls.' "

"Customary or not, at least it's more comforting than what's written in my insurance policy."

"My God, Howard, don't tell me you aren't covered for your accident!"

"I think I am. But I'll be hanged if I can figure out exactly how much I'm covered for. You ever read your

94

car insurance? It makes the Cabala look like a nursery rhyme. I don't know who they hire to write these mysteries."

"The same lawyers they hire to write 'employee contracts – at rabbinical level.' "

Both men chuckled, then Shulman turned serious. "Howard, this is probably as good a time as any to tell you what's on my mind."

"Don't tell me," Howard cut in, smiling, "I'll tell you. It's time we got ourselves a lawyer. Right?"

"Right."

Gone was the caution that characterized their early dialogues. Shulman and Roher resolved that if drown they must, then drown they would – together.

For several minutes they raked and sifted their individual legal connections in their search for a suitable attorney.

"What about Sam Cooperman?" Roher suggested. "You've known him ever since your first days here. That's a good twenty years."

"I'm afraid Samuel Cooperman is over the hill these days. In fact, he's over several hills. Besides, his credentials are more than a little tarnished now, thanks to Mr. Derek Hollenberg. Ah, youth...so efficient...so cruel!"

"Youth ... youth ..." Roher closed his eyes tightly as if praying. "We need somebody young, but not too young ..."

Both rabbis were thinking hard.

"There's that young lawyer Aaron Somebody who spoke to the Sisterhood back in the spring about women's rights." Roher said.

"He's too young," Shulman responded. "Anyway, there's plenty of women's rights around here already."

"How about that hotshot criminal lawyer, David Mulroney, or Mahoney. They say he's got a brain like an animal trap, and a mouth to match."

"Really, Howard!" Shulman pretended to be shocked. "We're not the Mafia, you and I. Besides, Mulroney, or Mahoney or whatever his name is belongs outside the territory. I don't think you and I, of all people, should be importing legal aid. We would only end up compounding the public exposure of this mess. With all due respect to our supporters on the board, they shouldn't have retained Gordon Clarkson. His tactics have only served to spread the fire. Besides, despite all the talk about gentile outsiders being useful because they are objective, I don't think they have a ... a feel for the unique and peculiar tensions of Jewish life." Shulman paused, then with a crafty smile he said: "Another important reason for not picking an outsider occurs to me ... the cost factor."

"Ah," said Roher, "I almost forgot about that."

"The way I figure it," Shulman mused, "if we can find us a reasonably good lawyer right under this very roof, someone 'in the family' so to speak, we'd probably be better off. And who knows, if it turns out to be someone you and I have miraculously avoided antagonizing all these years, someone we haven't offended or whose conscience we haven't pricked ... well, he just might be a little lenient in the matter of legal fees. And I don't know about you, Brother Roher, but speaking for myself, a little leniency would come in mighty handy ... just so long as it's not tied in with Rachel Mannheim's precious cost-of-living index."

More raking and sifting. This one was much too busy (and consequently infamous for turning out sloppy work); that one wasn't busy enough (for the very reason that he invariably turned out sloppy work from the day he was called to the bar); another had been too friendly with Rachel Mannheim's late husband. A fourth candidate, though he was now in his sixties, still insisted upon reliving the Spanish Civil War in which he'd fought with a Canadian contingent on the Loyalist side. To him even a rainy day was a Fascist conspiracy. Who could count on a lawyer like that for anything more than, say, a nice easy search of title or the swearing of a routine affidavit?

"There's another name that comes to mind," Roher said. "Hershel Brahms."

"Who?"

"Brahms. I think he calls himself Hershy."

"I repeat," Shulman said. "Who's he? Have I seen him at the temple?"

"Possibly. His wife is Charlotte Brahms. I think you married them some years ago. Their son, Kevin, is in my bar mitzvah enrichment program. Very bright kid. Has outrageous opinions on everything. Life of the class. Mrs. Brahms does a lot of work for Sisterhood, and I think she's also been active for many years on one committee or another around the temple. You *must* know Charlotte."

"Ah yes," Shulman said. "Of course ... Charlotte Zimmerman. I always seem to remember her best by her maiden name. I think she was in my first confirmation class here. I've caught sight of him a few times over the years at the tennis club, but I don't think I've seen him twice around here since the day he stepped on the lightbulb under the chupah. A lot of broken glass has gone underfoot since then. What do you know about him?"

"I know that he drives a Mercedes. Keeps it polished like a piece of jewellery, too."

"Are those his only qualifications?" Shulman asked.

"Don't knock those qualifications," said Roher. "Remember, I believe in awarding high marks for good carmanship. I've run into him – figuratively, that is – a half dozen times or so in the parking lot."

"He's a 'parking-lot Jew' then," Shulman said. "I know the kind. They make it a point never to switch off their engines. Drop the kids and run, and don't look back or you're liable to turn into a pillar of the community."

"Yes, I suppose he's that kind."

Shulman looked skeptical. "It doesn't sound to me as if he's a likely prospect."

"On the contrary, he may be ideal," Roher protested. "Look at it this way," he went on. "Firstly, he's Jewish. Secondly, he's 'in the family' as you put it, even though he seldom comes in from the parking lot. Thirdly, because of his very position way out there on the periphery, it may well be that he's completely uninvolved in the powerplay between the Mannheimers and the anti-Mannheimers. So there you have it: uninvolved, unfettered, uncluttered. What could be better for you and me?"

Shulman was not sold; not yet. "The Mercedes bothers me. He must be expensive."

"That's possible. We'd have to lay our cards on the table with him about fees."

"The fundamental question, of course, is: does he know any law?"

"He must," insisted Roher. "Scuttlebutt has it that he's an income tax and estate-planning expert. Anybody who can read The Income Tax Act has to be something more than a well-trained orangoutang."

"From whence cometh that scuttlebutt, may I ask?"

"From an unimpeachable source ... namely Kevin Brahms."

Shulman looked astonished. "Out of the mouth of a babe you're willing to accept a recommendation about a matter as important as choosing a lawyer?"

"Kevin is no ordinary babe."

"A son's pride in his father is hardly an unimpeachable source."

"I've heard talk as well at the odd Brotherhood breakfast. Also Mrs. Isaacs – I'm speaking of the late Moe Isaacs' widow – apparently she doesn't clip a toenail, let alone a coupon, before checking with Hershy Brahms, and I needn't remind you about the kind of prima donna Sonya Isaacs can be."

"No indeed, you needn't remind me," said Shulman. He remembered the day Moe Isaacs' body was found at the foot of Tamara Towers, remembered the elaborate funeral, and the widow's sentimental insistence that Shulman deliver the bulk of Moe's eulogy in Yiddish, a language her husband hadn't set foot in since his childhood in Poland.

Shulman brightened. "Well now, if this fellow Brahms is sharp enough for the congregation's wealthiest dowager, maybe ... yes, he might be worth contacting at this point."

"Perhaps you should give Brahms a call then," said Roher. "After all, you're the senior man. Besides, you confirmed Charlotte Brahms, married the couple, and I assume you named their son."

"On the contrary," Shulman said, "perhaps *you* should call him. The two of you have so much more in common ... you both drive foreign cars."

It was a typical Sunday morning at the residence of Charlotte and Hershy Brahms. Louis Brahms, looking windblown, had just come in through the side door, followed by a dozen reddish maple leaves that had been playing ring-around-the-rosy in the driveway.

Hershy pretended to be annoyed. "Why must you always use the tradesmen's entrance?"

"Front doors are for guests. Relatives and dead leaves use the side door. Here, take this for Chrisake before I drop dead." Louis Brahms uncradled a large white paper bag bearing in bold blue letters "Glicksman's Hearth-to-Table Coffee Shops."

"Charlotte," Hershy called to the kitchen, "the Jewish Santa Claus is here again ... the one with the blue and white bag ..."

"That's right, petzel, make fun," Louis scolded. "But remember, blue and white, that's our people's colours. Some day God will punish you."

Charlotte emptied the contents of the bag: an assortment of bagels and rolls, and enough sliced bread to pave an airport.

"That'll do for breakfast," Hershy said, "but how 'bout lunch and dinner?"

"Lunch and dinner's *your* headache. Why do you

99

think I gave you an expensive education? ... Where's Kevin?"

Hershy checked his watch. "At this very moment your grandson is being inculcated."

Louis' face twisted instantly into an anguished frown. The thought of his grandson having so much as a head-cold opened gaping wounds in his heart. "Inculcated! My God, what is it, measles or what?"

"Inculcated, not inoculated," Charlotte said.

Louis glanced from Charlotte to Hershy, then back to Charlotte. "Will somebody please tell me what's going on?" he pleaded.

"He's getting religion," Hershy said.

"Kevin's at the temple," Charlotte added, "and everything's fine. He got a lift so he doesn't have to cross Bathurst Street. He's also getting a lift home so he doesn't have to cross Bathurst Street again. Now stop worrying, Dad, and eat."

She set before him his favourite Sunday morning dish – Nova Scotia lox with onions done up in an omelette. She also saw to it that there was a juice glass of vodka for him on the table. Downing the vodka in a single gulp, Louis exhaled a deep growl of contentment that had its origins somewhere in the steppes of Russia. "You know what they used to call vodka in the old country?" he said. "Peasant's-breath, that's what they called it. You could buy a whole trainload of peasant's-breath for a lousy pouch of tobacco. In America they line up and pay six-eighty a bottle, and give it high-society names ... Bloodydriver, Screwmary ... You'll see, at Kevin's bar mitzvah ninety-nine percent of your fency-shmency friends will be drinking that green chazerai with the foamy stuff on top ... I think they call 'em giblets—"

"They call 'em gimlets, and they're made with gin," Hershy interrupted. "Incidentally, who says we're having our fency-shmency friends to Kevin's bar mitzvah?"

Louis looked shocked. "What are you telling me, you're gonna have a bar mitzvah on the quiet, nobody should show up? What're you running, a celebration or a military secret?"

Charlotte, looking thoroughly dejected, sighed, "God only knows."

Louis sensed immediately he'd led the discussion into a war zone. He peered sternly over his eyeglasses at his son. "So, Hershy, what's this? You're making life difficult these days for my one-and-only daughter?"

"It's Sunday morning, Dad. Time to talk about your estate," Hershy said, trying to keep the conversation light.

The typical Sunday morning tabletalk centred around Louis Brahms' estate and whether or not he should make a new will. "The Rites of Sunday," Hershy called it. From the inside breast pocket of his jacket Louis would withdraw a small notebook with a well-worn leatherette cover. Hershy would tap the side of his coffeecup with a spoon, and announce in a portentous voice: "Quiet please, we are now going to have The Reading Of The List."

"Sure, sure, that's right . . . call me crazy."

"Who's calling you crazy? Nobody's calling you crazy."

"This is a very serious business, Hershy."

"I know, Dad, I know. I just realized it's been a whole month since you made a new will!"

Louis would stall, like a child waiting to be coaxed to recite for a visitor, and Charlotte would put her arm around Louis' shoulder. "C'mon Dad, read us The List. We want to hear it again, honest."

"We're dying to hear it," Hershy would assure him.

Milking his own persecution to the last drop, Louis would shake his index finger at his son. "Go on, laugh now, but someday, when I'm fertilizing the cemetery, you'll count the dividend cheques and the rent cheques, and believe me, will you say a kaddish-and-a-half for your old man! It isn't easy in this world to accumulate an estate. And why do you think I do it? For you. What else?"

"Read already!" Hershy would command, barely able to conceal his amusement at the absurdity that was about to commence.

"All right. All right ... don't holler on me."

A final dramatic pause. Then the elder Brahms would clear his throat ceremoniously and begin: "As of three p.m. Friday, when the market closed, my thousand shares Consolidated Durite was two seventy a share; that's up. Twenty-five hundred McDonald Tool closed at three ten, unchanged. I still got a thousand National Eastern Freightlines they should rot in hell it's down eight points to six dollars ninety-nine ..."

On it went. Some two dozen stocks and bonds, a fistful of second mortgages, and three or four small buildings near the corner of Eglinton and Bathurst Streets showing an average return of fourteen percent (net). "Not bad for a fiddle-player from Kamensk-Podolsk," Louis would say, summing up.

Of course there was always an undertone of fear.

"Another Chinese restaurant is moving near me on Eglinton Avenue. Pretty soon there won't be a China-man left downtown. They're all moving up North with us. Where we go, they go. It's like Ruth and what's-her-name in the Bible."

"Don't worry, it'll be great for business," said Hershy. "Think of all those Chinese families in Forest Hill sending out for Jewish food on Sunday nights."

"Even when it comes to Jewish food they'll stick with their own. You know something, the House of Wang is now advertising on a big sign in the window: 'Latkes and Blintzes Our Specialty.' Right across the street from me, the bastards."

And then there was the bleak black presence of Ottawa in Louis Brahms' life. "Ottawa" examining and re-examining his tax returns going all the way back to the Garden of Eden; "Ottawa" continually demanding that columns be totalled, squares checkmarked and blanks filled; "Ottawa" hovering like a vulture over near-carrion as Louis grew older and the title to all his possessions eroded with uncertainty. All these worldly goods ... his, but somehow not his. True enough, the legal documents called him owner, landlord, and yet Louis never succeeded in overcoming the feeling that he was no better than a tenant – a born tenant at that, a man who would be a rentpayer until that final day on earth when his lease would expire.

How to preserve for his son all that he'd accumulated, that was the challenge. That was the reason for the Rites of Sunday. See the estate father left ... nice, tidy, intact like a virgin. If Louis Brahms could never earn immortality, that was all right; he was satisfied to settle for temporary immortality – a funeral attended by a decent number of people, a month or two of reduced social commitments on the part of his heirs, perhaps a framed picture of himself hung directly over the framed dollar bill on the wall next to the cash register. *The main thing was: Hang onto as much as possible!* "Beat Ottawa" – that was the name of the game.

But this morning the normal order of business was interrupted. Louis scowled at his son. "My estate can wait. About it we'll talk later. Meanwhile listen to me. You know I never mix in where I shouldn't in your personal life. By me that's an absolute one hundred procent rule. On the other hand I'm your father so I got a right to know. Is there something wrong between you two?"

"You'd better tell him, Hershy," Charlotte said.

Hershy explained that Shulman and Roher had called on him to act as their counsel, not only to protect their contractual rights, but to sue Mrs. Mannheim and a number of her more prominent supporters for damages. In reaction to the earlier advertisement, the pro-Mannheim group had placed their own advertisement – a full page also – in the *Canadian Jewish Times*. This piece acknowledged that there was indeed a power struggle, but intimated that the whole affair had been carefully engineered by the rabbis in retaliation for Rachel Mannheim's refusal to go along with their excessive salary demands. What especially infuriated the rabbis was that their ideological difference with Mrs. Mannheim went unmentioned, leaving the distinct impression with readers that here were two men of the cloth whose chief concern was to eat now and pray later. As far as Shulman and Roher were concerned, the advertisement, though couched in Derek Hollenberg's guarded prose style, was plainly defamatory. There was only one way to respond – in a court of law.

In an unguarded moment, Roher made known his feelings to St. Clair Graydon, a well-known radio personality who made a practice of scanning the local ethnic press for off-beat gossip and had chanced upon the offending advertisement. Despite the "St." in Graydon's given name, he was an avowed atheist and nothing gave him greater pleasure than to report public pratfalls from grace of supposedly sacrosanct individuals and institutions. In his supper-hour newscast that evening Graydon teased his listeners: "Here's a tasty Jewish appetizer, and for a change it ain't chopped liver ... What fashionable house of worship is about to lock rams-horns with its two rabbis in a major lawsuit? My informant – let's just say it's a voice that came to me from a burning bush in the north end of the city – tells me the case involves everything from complicated breaches of contract to the Vietnam War and, believe-it-or-not, The Four Freedoms! We'll have more developments in this unique and bizarre temple turmoil ... so tune in tomorrow, same time, same burning bush ..."

Graydon's audience invariably included the city editors of the local dailies. They quickly sensed that beyond the hors d'oeuvres just broadcast lay a feast of greater magnitude and depth than even a veteran journalist like St. Clair Graydon could imagine. By next afternoon the front pages of Toronto's newspapers carried accounts of the impending court battle, emphasizing in prominent headlines what they regarded as basic human rights issues. One headline read: "First The Chicago Seven, Now The Toronto Two." These reports suggested that Mrs. Mannheim was seeking to clamp a lid on the rabbis' freedom to speak out on social issues, particularly the iniquitous war in Vietnam; that they were being deprived of their rights to question a secret report critical of their leadership; that they were denied full opportunity to negotiate their contracts.

Not to be outdone, television networks planted camera crews on the sidewalks outside the synagogue. Viewers of late-night television news watched endless footage of delivery vans rolling in and out of the temple parking lot, giving the impression that somehow the cabal involved the Teamsters Union, but the ominous voices of the on-the-spot reporters left no doubt that within its tall granite walls, one of the country's oldest and largest Jewish institutions was being torn apart.

A nationally-syndicated columnist, who sided with the Mannheimers, saw all these goings-on as further evidence of the failing separation of church and state. "A clergyman's place is in the pulpit," the columnist declared, "and not in those forums ordinarily inhabited by politicians." An editorial in the country's largest newspaper castigated both sides: "In this year 1969, or 5729 in the Hebrew calendar, we've witnessed one giant step on the moon for mankind, and several gigantic leaps backward here on earth."

Like bad weather, the temple controversy crossed the United States border, exciting the attention of several liberal rabbinical unions who banded together and, in a sharp letter of rebuke to Mrs. Mannheim, reminded her that precedents existed for the boycotting of any congregation which dealt unjustly with its spiritual leaders. A group of Protestant ministers sent a telegram of support to Shulman and Roher and promptly published it as well in the form of an open letter to the temple board of directors. A former Roman Catholic priest took time off from organizing anti-war demonstrations in California to praise the two rabbis "way up there in Canada" during an appearance on a late-night talk show. *Time* assigned its Religion editors to follow the story. In the pages of *Newsweek* a staff pundit, perhaps wishfully, conjured up a vision of Shulman and Roher nailing a set of ninety-five revolutionary theses to the temple door. And further south, in the mountains of Mexico, an internationally renowned philosopher, viewing the schism from his cultural eyrie, composed a lengthy letter to the New York *Times* advocating the "de-clergying" of religion.

Scandalized by all this publicity, Jewish community leaders urged the antagonists to consider compromises and to avoid at all costs dragging the issues before the courts. Offers to mediate poured in, but these were rejected by both sides who regarded the would-be mediators in most cases as lacking impartiality or competence. But had a mediator of acknowledged impartiality and competence appeared on the scene, it is doubtful that he or she would have succeeded, for the crisis was no longer merely a matter of religion and ethics; it had developed into the most fundamental matter known to any warrior – the preservation of his or her own reputation.

Louis smiled. "A lawyer for rabbis all of a sudden?" Despite the little contact Louis Brahms had over the years with Rabbis Shulman and Roher - or any rabbis, for that matter – he felt a certain pride in the thought of his son entering an arena to be their champion. "A lawyer for rabbis, eh?" he mused.

"Well, not quite. I told them I wanted to think it over."

"What's to think over? You're a lawyer, no? A case is a case."

"You make it sound like a game of gin rummy. Anyway, the whole thing's really not in my line, Dad. What's involved here goes far beyond my little realm of expertise ... synagogue politics, budgets, religion."

"Politics you know already; you've been voting since you're twenty-one. Budgets? All you gotta know is how to add two columns and make it come out even, which thank God you know. And when it comes to religion —"

"Oh God," Hershy broke in, laughing, "you're not going to tell me I'm an expert there, too!"

"Okay, let's be honest about it ..." Louis turned to Charlotte and continued: "As far as religious business is concerned, about all I ever taught Hershy was how to pick a two-year-old and pray that she likes a muddy track. I admit it. But from what I read in the papers, what's going on at your temple isn't exactly made in heaven, so I don't think a fella's got to be a chief rabbi or even a pope to understand it. Louis turned back to Hershy. "Myself I think you should call the rabbis and you should say sure I'll take the case, it'll be an honour. Also Hershy, it'll make your little wife happy, and I want my only daughter should be happy."

Louis smiled affectionately at his daughter-in-law. He was aware of her attachment to the temple, and equally aware of her disappointment in him over the years. Perhaps because Louis Brahms had been born in Russia, had undergone the rigours of an eastern European cheder, and spoke Yiddish much of the time, Charlotte had looked to him to play the role of patriarch. Art Zimmerman, Charlotte's father, certainly lacked proper credentials. A native of Detroit, he had emigrated to Toronto as a small boy, and knew less Yiddish than one could find in the average delicatessen menu. Moreover, he was a hypochondriac. (Kevin's moments of closeness with Grandpa Zimmerman consisted of fetching pills and glasses of water and listening to the man's complaints.)

Louis Brahms, in Charlotte's eyes the one man in the family possessing the potential for venerability, had failed, and he knew it. Here was a possibility for him to put matters right. To Hershy he said: "Don't even wait till tomorrow. Call 'em today. I say you should, and Charlotte says so too, don't you Charlotte?"

Charlotte stared into her empty coffeecup. "Charlotte?" Louis called to her gently. "Tell him he should do this ... for his sake, and for yours. And who knows, maybe even for mine ... Charlotte?"

Charlotte's lips barely moved. "I can't."

Louis sat up, astonished. "What?"

"I'm sorry, I can't."

"But ... but ... I don't understand. All these years you kept coaxing Hershy ... What's happened all of a sudden?"

Hershy started to reply: "What's happened, Dad, is —"

Angrily Charlotte cut in. "Dammit Hershy, I can tell him. I have a tongue in my head too."

Charlotte looked intently at her father-in-law, saw the confusion in his eyes, the pained expression around his mouth, his long bony violinist's fingers fumbling with his placemat, and knew that at this moment he was reliving earlier days, past explosions, and past sinkings of hope.

"I'm sorry, Dad, but there's something you don't understand. Let me explain. You see, the President of the temple – Rachel Mannheim – well, she and I have worked together closely for a number of years. We served on all sorts of committees together; the very first time she was nominated for the board I seconded the motion; and I was one of the five people who signed her nomination form when she ran for president. After her election she asked me to prepare a special report for her on membership retention ... you know, attendance at services, that kind of thing. I'm afraid my report wasn't too favourable to the rabbis. In fact, it's become a very sore point with them. To this day I don't think they know who wrote it, but sooner or later they may find out. So you see, Dad, if Hershy becomes the rabbis' legal counsel, it will place me in an extremely awkward position ... in fact, an impossible position." Charlotte paused. "I hope you understand now."

Louis closed his eyes, the better to review in his mind the words just spoken. His lips moved slightly and he nodded his head, as if he were debating with himself. Without opening his eyes he said: "Hershy, you going along with this?"

"I don't see that I have any choice."

"You knew about the report?"

"Yes, everybody's heard about it. But I didn't know Charlotte had written it until I told her about the rabbis' call."

"Will you have to tell them about Charlotte?" Louis asked.

"Of course. If I were to accept them as clients, I'd be bound ethically to tell them."

"And I suppose it works out very nice and convenient for you, yes?"

"I don't quite get what you mean."

"I mean you got your 'out.' Thanks to Charlotte you got a good excuse to get yourself off the hook, like they say."

"I was never *on* the hook."

Louis opened his eyes. "Oh yes you were, godammit! The minute that phone rang you were on the hook, sonny-boy."

Hershy glowered at his father. "What the hell are you talking about?"

"I'm talking about being a mensch."

"Look," Hershy yelled angrily, "aside from the problem of Charlotte's position in all this, do you have even the faintest notion of how complicated the problems are at the temple? This isn't that two-by-four fleabag we used to sit and sweat to death in downtown when I was a kid. We're into the big time here. This is the Carnegie Hall of the synagogue trade. To some people it's damn near the nation's capitol. Anyway, I don't see why I should get drawn into the meat grinder. You always succeeded in staying clear of it. I lost count of how many times you checked out early because the synagogue made you feel like you were choking to death."

"What was for me doesn't necessarily have to be for you," Louis said.

"History repeats itself, Dad."

"Not all history — only some. If it was otherwise, nobody would need tomorrow."

"There are a lot of challenges I can think of that are worth pursuing, but you'd have to go a helluva long way to convince me that this is one of them.'

"Oh, I see," Louis said. "So what *is* a worthwhile challenge in your eyes? To do like that Norwegian fella which I forget his name — the one you've been blabbing about for months? To stick yourself in a homemade boat and go around in circles on the ocean until they find you and the whole kit and caboodle inside some whale's belly and by golly look at that … it's what's left of Hershy Brahms! That, by you, is an achievement?"

"Why the hell not?"

"Because it's not for a Jew, that's why!"

"Are you seriously trying to convince me," Hershy said, "that dreams are restricted … like beaches used to be when I was a kid? 'Christians Only Permitted To Dream Here?' "

"Exactly."

"But this is 1969."

"I don't give a damn if it's 2069! I don't give a damn if you got ten fancy German cars in your garage and a kitchen loaded up to the ceiling with pork chops … the fact is, when it comes to dreams you got to dream Jewish."

Sarcastically Hershy said: "I suppose it's a proper dream for a Jew to hire himself out to a couple of rabbis so they can sue the very people they blessed only a few weeks ago? You'd really admire me for that, wouldn't you? It would make you very proud, no doubt."

110

"Put the way you put it, no. There is nothing to be proud about when Jews grab each other by the throat. But your job could be to put them together again. You got the training, the talent. Thank God, you're very successful ... people know you, they know your ability."

"I swore never to get involved in that kind of thing."

"When did you swear?"

"Years ago ... after you quit your synagogue."

"Then it's time to *un*swear, Hershy."

"It's not that simple. Remember, there's Charlotte to think about."

"Charlotte's a big girl," Louis said. "She can handle herself ... can't you Charlotte?"

Charlotte pushed her chair back from the table. She was desperate to escape to the kitchen. "I'll make some more coffee," she said quietly. She rose and reached for the coffeepot. Instantly Louis' hand was on her arm, restraining her. "No," he said firmly, "I'd like you to sit, Charlotte. There's something I have to say, and I want both of you to hear it."

Charlotte sank slowly back in her chair.

"I know – believe me I know – what's going on here ..." Louis' voice began to tremble. "I recognize it, because I saw it before, once a long long time ago ... although I never imagined in my worst nightmares it could happen again." Looking straight into Hershy's eyes, Louis continued: "The truth, Hershy, is that you have inherited your mother's disease. I don't know how ... but it's so. Your mother, rest in peace, ate herself up alive in a dream. She dreamed she was Charles Lindbergh's wife. And while she was alive I thought, well, it's a case of infatuation over a hero ... that's the big word your Uncle Max called it – infatuation. Too bad, I thought, but that's it. But after Goldie died I kept thinking about it and thinking about it. And I asked myself why did she marry me ... *me* of all people? And then, it came to me. When we first met I must have looked to her more like a Russian or a Swede than a

Jew. And who knows, forty years ago, if not from the front then maybe from behind I looked a little like Lindbergh."

"I don't see what this has to do with me," Hershy said. "I'm not suffering from any disease."

"Not from a disease that gives you spots, or a fever that burns you up, but believe me, Hershy, there's an infection deep inside you. You have to understand something: you see, the first time I laid eyes on your mother she was dancing a fraylich and I thought to myself now there's a girl what's got a Jewish soul; that's how perfect she did that dance. But I could tell after a month or two that it was only a show. Already she was in her new job with MacInnis the member of parliament and the disease was working. Pretty soon there was not even a show ... nothing ... that's how fast it worked. The disease was ... she wished she wasn't a Jew."

Hershy looked incredulous. "I don't believe my ears! Are you accusing me of being an anti-Semite?"

"I didn't say you're an anti-Semite. I said you wish you could get out of being Jewish. There's a big difference. An anti-Semite would like to kill others, and sometimes he does and sometimes he doesn't. But a Jew who can't stand to be what he is *for sure* kills himself."

"Since when are you a psychiatrist?'

"I don't have to be a psychiatrist. I lived long enough with poor Goldie ... A person gets to know these things."

"Thanks for the free diagnosis," Hershy said, "but when I'm ready to have the garbage in my head carried out, I'll hire a shrink to do it at fifty bucks an hour."

Abruptly Louis stood and threw down his napkin. For the first time in Hershy's memory, the older Brahms' pale Slavic eyes looked white and cold, like a Russian winter.

"A head doctor can't help you, Hershy," Louis said hoarsely. "You're already a dying man."

Leaving Charlotte and Hershy in silence at the diningroom table, he strode out of the house without another word.

Later that afternoon Hershy lay sprawled on the sofa in the den, the lower half of his body buried under the Sunday edition of the New York *Times*, the front page of which carried a two-column feature story under the headline: "HEYERDAHL PREPARES FOR SECOND EXPERIMENTAL VOYAGE NEXT MAY." Above the headline was a map of the South Atlantic, showing the ocean currents as swirling arrows and a snaky dotted line extending from Safi to the Barbados, marking the route.

Nearby, on the coffee table, stood the remains of a small pitcher of martinis mixed an hour earlier as the sun began its early descent in the autumn sky. Intended as a substitute for the fading daylight, the martinis hadn't worked and what was left of them was mostly icewater by now. Through the louvered doors that separated den from kitchen Hershy could hear the muffled sounds of pots and pans and the squeak of the oven door from time to time. Charlotte was going all out ... standing-rib roast, candied sweet potatoes, apple pie ... intended as a culinary antidote to Hershy's Sunday evening blahs. Bless her, it wouldn't work either – he knew that in advance.

This was no ordinary case of Sunday blahs. This was the Sunday Hershy Brahms' father – the same man who, forty years earlier, had given him life – pronounced him a dying man. Hershy stared out the den window at a tangled network of bare maple branches. With more than a little envy, he asked himself: "What makes the old man so damned sure of himself?" Why, he pondered, did Louis' natural wellsprings continue to irrigate and give new life, while his own regularly narrowed to a mere trickle and seemed forever on the verge of running dry?

I *must* be a better man than my father, Hershy

insisted to himself. Just as he must surely be a better man than his father was. Just as Kevin must someday be better than I. If sons didn't turn out better than their fathers, where the hell was there any momentum to life? What the hell was the point to living?

I *must* be a better man than my father, Hershy said, and repeated it over and over, hypnotizing himself until, through the window, the maple branches turned to a blur; he could feel his eyelids fluttering (was it the martinis at last?) and all the news that was fit to print that day became weightless across his lower legs, and he knew he was drifting ... drifting forward into the month of May in the following year ...

A new log book. On the cover in large block letters: "The Journal of Ra II." Crisp blank pages unstained by seaspray or grubby fingerprints, ready to accept the first hopeful entries of the new voyage.

Some ten months have passed since Hershy Brahms broke the tie among the crewmen by voting to abandon Ra I. "The boat dies ... the crew lives; that is the proper order of things," Hershy had murmured to himself in the rubber dinghy as they rowed toward the rescue yacht. There was a faint though unmistakeable hint of contempt in the Russian's voice when he said: "... they always choose life." Secretly however, the Russian was relieved that an ultimate act of heroism (or foolishness?) had been postponed. That day, clambering aboard the yacht, perhaps the Russian dreamt only of a sunlit promenade in Leningrad. And what of the Spaniard, the Arab, the Japanese, the Frenchman? Each must have had his own sunlit promenade somewhere, or a quiet strip of white beach, or a very private back garden, with cool bottles of white wine and ripe velvety raspberries and a woman bending sleeveless to be caressed on the shoulders ...

And yet, ten months later the women are kissed goodbye, the flowers, the wine, the fruit are set aside, discarded – like playthings that have been outgrown. On the wharf at Safi the men gather once again, saluting their Norwegian captain with mock naval formality, jesting about storms and sharks. All hands present and accounted for. All ... except one. Where is the Jew? Where is the chap in the Hathaway shirt who had such a craving for the sea, who wanted nothing more than a mat to squat upon in the low cabin of the papyrus boat, who was content to eat cold food out of earthenware jars and perform his clumsy ablutions hanging over the side of the craft? Heyerdahl and the others wait. The jesting ceases, impatience creeps in. The Spaniard glances at his watch. "Where the hell is he?" he mutters tersely. "Don't worry," says the Frenchman, "he'll be along any minute now. They're always late. Being late is their national vice."

But Brahms hasn't overlooked the hour, nor has he been detained by some circumstance beyond his control. No ... Hershy Brahms is thinking things over.

When this expedition is finished the Japanese will retire to the creative solitude of his darkroom. Perhaps he will produce a book of dramatic pictures depicting the brave days of Ra I and Ra II, or a documentary that wins prizes at international film festivals. Possibly he will invent a faster shutter, a more waterproof lens. Afterward, he will roam his native islands contemplating nature through the viewfinder of his camera, photographing flower arrangements and shrines, and will have no difficulty at all finding in those serene subjects his reason for being.

The Arab will sail and sail again, for the blood coursing through his arteries is mixed with ocean currents. And yet, when the salty taste of boredom or fear becomes too much for his mouth, the wide-open deserts of the Middle East will always be his for the asking.

The Frenchman will settle down in Paris, secure once again among all the magnificent arches and monuments and palaces that proclaim his people's permanence.

And the Scandinavian will travel the world lecturing about epic struggles between man and nature but will always find peace at home ... home in Norway, among the mountains and fjords that have for centuries rested virtually undisturbed in the possession of his race.

What awaits Hershy Brahms, Diaspora Dweller, on his return to Toronto after this expedition?

Will he drive his Mercedes up and down University Avenue? Walk the streets of Yorkville inspecting artists' pricetags? Draft documents that begin: "This is the Last Will and Testament of me, Hyman Eliezer Rosenzweig?" Reinstate his membership in a service club and raffle off a new Chevrolet? ...

Or will he seek to rise above all that and present himself to the public at large as a new phenomenon – the Jewish hero of exploration, the man who left his knotty-pine recreation room far behind for an uncomfortable reed raft, just to prove an historical fact?

Journalists will interview him; yes, he will appear on television as a mystery guest on a panel show, and – who knows? – an athletic club, which has hitherto withheld it lavish facilities from the likes of Hershy Brahms, may invite him to swim in its indoor pool.

Ah, but then how does he fare when he, a Jew, gathers among other Jews? How does all this help him? More importantly, how does all this help him when he is by himself?

"Where is he?" the Spaniard cries. Heyerdahl and the others shade their eyes from the blazing African sun and scan the crowd on the beach, expecting any moment to see Brahms burst through breathlessly.

A full hour past the scheduled departure time, and still no Hershy Brahms. Nor will there be ... not today ... not tomorrow ... perhaps not even in the year 2069. Ra I had confirmed his will to live. Ra II can give him nothing now, nothing that matters. He knows that now. In Hershy Brahms' life there are certain priorities that require immediate attention.

Brahms, Chooser of Life, must now embark on a

trickier and more hazardous voyage. He must discover how to go on living where he is, with the things that make sense and the things that are crazy, with the lovable and the detestable, the genuine and the false . . .

Suddenly the branches of the maple came into focus again and Charlotte was calling to him from the diningroom. For Hershy Brahms, Diaspora Dweller, the fantasies of Ra I and Ra II had come to an end.

On the following Sunday, Hershy Brahms missed the ritual Sunday brunch. Instead, he found himself in the temple boardroom, seated at the long walnut directors' table between Rabbi Shulman and Rabbi Roher. Opposite him sat Rachel Mannheim and next to her Derek Hollenberg, the latter looking as crisp and rectangular as a new attaché case.

"May we begin?" Rachel Mannheim asked.

"We're ready if you are," replied Brahms.

Hershy Brahms was in it.

In it up to his eyeballs.

May 1, 1976: Continental Europe is bracing itself for yet another invasion by England's flamboyant Rolling Stones who begin their 1976 tour later this month. In a logistical operation reminiscent of D-Day at Normandy, the Stones will cross the English Channel with thirteen truckloads of electrical equipment, musical instruments (including Keith Richard's eighteen guitars) and a $70,000 wardrobe worn by Mick Jagger. Noted for doing everything on a grand scale, the Stones last year gave forty-five concerts in twenty-seven cities during their whirlwind North American tour, grossing about $13 million. The trenchant irony that characterized their music in the sixties has now taken on a new intensity through their expanding use of spectacular stage and sound effects, and audiences around the globe are responding in record numbers. Last summer 200,000 fans showed up at a single concert in England ...

Three

From the awninged terrace the young man was able to see much of the bay of St. Jean Cap Ferrat, although the villas and apartment buildings on the far shore stood out against an almost white sky as little more than a pink mass undefined except for their outline. One knew on faith that, on this very June morning in 1976, the far shore existed – as did the near shore – as a refuge from the merciless inland heat for thousands of natives and tourists. Yet, concealed by haze, the humanity broiling on the beaches across the water could just as likely have been dead as alive; nothing seemed to be stirring there. In the bay hundreds of cruisers, sailboats and smaller craft lay anchored, like dormant cats. It occurred to the young man that never before, not even in Florida or Nassau or Southern California, had he ever beheld a scene in which everything – land, water, sky, buildings, people – appeared to have been cooked through and through.

A large yacht, incredibly large, the largest he'd ever seen, with a navy blue hull and a small helicopter roosting on its afterdeck, began to move, heading slowly, silently toward the mouth of the bay. The young man's eyes followed the yacht and for a moment he was at the wheel, calling to the steward for another gin and tonic. "And another for mam'selle, Henri." From the main salon the bikinied girl called, "Bart darling, it's the phone ... L.A..." The line from Los Angeles was remarkably clear (a miracle of communication? Hell no; Bart Brahms had the finest goddamn ship-to-shore equipment on the seas – thirty thousand dollars' worth!).

The voice on the line gave him a rundown of the day's messages. Bob called. He's in New York if you want to reach him. Joni called and left her number in Chicago. Stevie will be in L.A. at The Beverly Hills for a few days this coming week. Also heard from: Simpson from the Bank, Forster from J. Walter Thompson, Hamp Brethour from C.B.S. about a special this winter with Bob and Joni, and is Baez available?

Orders: Tell Dylan the decision's yes. No, wait, I'll call him myself. I'll get Joni in Chicago later, maybe Tuesday or Wednesday. Tell Mike Dacey to look after Stevie... I don't care what it costs, the sky's the limit now that Stevie's new album is topping the charts. Tell Simpson to go fuck himself; he's got enough security on that loan to choke a dinosaur. Wait ... Tell Mike Dacey to take him to lunch at Chasen's, Simp loves Chasen's, also I think he's got a crush on Mike... Forster can wait... Hamp Brethour? Tell him I don't know yet. If he wants me he knows where to reach me ... No, not tonight; I ran into David Niven yesterday in Beaulieu and we're having dinner ...

The dark blue yacht came to a sudden stop not more than a few hundred yards from where it had been moored. Perhaps it was just too bloody hot to venture out on the Mediterranean. Perhaps the owner simply wanted a better vantage point from which to train his ten-power binoculars on the bare-breasted women on the beach below the terrace, especially the one in the leopard-pattern bikini spreading Bain de Soleil all over her exposed bosom under the red and orange umbrella. But it wasn't the sight of the leopard woman that fascinated Bart; rather it was the possibility of who was on the bridge of the yacht that intrigued him. Who – who the hell would own a boat like that? Such questions opened the curtains of Bart's imagination – curtains which in this southern part of France closed, it seemed, for no more than a few brief minutes in the middle of the night when the density and richness of the day's scenery and food and people became too much for him and he dropped off to sleep, sated and exhausted.

"Christ, I gotta get outa here!" Bart said to himself. He felt as if he'd spent the last ten days living in a strip of overexposed film. My goddamn luck! he thought. The worst heatwave this country's had in over two hundred years, and I had to pick this summer to come. No matter where he'd found himself – whether it was on the open griddle of the Place Vendôme in Paris, or the treed square in the heart of Vichy, or at the water's edge at St. Jean Cap Ferrat, the heat stalked him like a mugger, cornering him, getting him down, robbing him of energy, leaving him breathless and immobile. "I gotta get outa here," he repeated.

A waiter approached from the bar at the far end of the terrace: "M'sieur?"

"Vous avez une table?" Bart asked.

The waited shrugged. They all shrug, Bart thought. In France it's the national sport – shrugging. They shrug singly, in pairs, they've even got a goddamn Olympic Shrug Team.

"Vous n'avez pas une table?"

The waiter gestured. See for yourself, his hands and shoulders said.

"Thanks a helluva lot," Bart muttered.

"M'sieur?"

"J'ai dit, merci beaucoup," Bart said much louder. His French was Grade 12, C-minus, but a month in France had demonstrated that speaking loudly to those foreigners somehow guaranteed comprehension even if it didn't cure defective grammar. The Frenchman gave Bart a dirty look, and returned to the bar. He'd understood.

"You may join us if you like."

Bart turned in the direction of the invitation. Down two tables – a girl, early twenties, long blond hair, perfect teeth, white t-shirt. Miss Scandinavia, Bart thought. Seated across from her a hairy ball of a man, about forty, old-fashioned metal-framed eyeglasses, swarthy complexion, collarless cotton blouse from India, everything about him – his clothes, his body parts – loose-fitting, spiritual (probably the girl's guru or yoga instructor). Bart hesitated; he wasn't sure if he was in the mood to meet strangers, make small talk. The damn heat, everything looking bleached. He pretended he hadn't heard.

"You can join us." This time it was the man calling.

God, Bart thought, here we go . . . an hour of leather-sandaled philosophizing. ("Tell me, honestly, do you *really* feel you've got your head together?" . . . "Yes, I *really* do, but thanks for being so concerned.")

The spiritual-looking one rose and motioned to Bart to take the empty chair next to him.

"Thanks," Bart said, "but I don't want to spoil your privacy."

"Please, we don't mind at all," the girl smiled.

Bart took the chair offered him, and sat facing the girl. The waiter returned and, without the slightest sign of interest, asked for Bart's order.

"I'd like the green salad and lemonade."

The waiter slouched, resting one hand on the table-top; otherwise he showed no reaction. There was something comic about his surliness, and Bart couldn't help being amused. To his new-found luncheon companions he said: "What's wrong, doesn't he like what I ordered?"

"It's more personal than that," the man replied. "He thinks you're an American." He nodded toward the girl. "You'd better let her order. She knows the magic words."

Rather curtly, the girl spoke to the waiter. "Salade verte, et un citron pressé." Then, bitingly, she added: "S'il vous plaît." Bart thought she spoke French like a native. The waiter nodded obediently and shuffled off toward the kitchen.

"I'm Norm Arvanitis," the hairy man said, "from Pittsburgh. This here's Katherine O'Hearn."

"Kathy," the girl corrected, firmly.

"What's wrong with Katherine?" asked Bart.

"Katherine sounds too institutional ... like Battleship Linoleum."

Bart liked her immediately. "I'm Bart Brahms ... Toronto." He looked at Kathy O'Hearn. "I figured you were Swedish or Finnish."

"Boston Irish. Sorry."

To Arvanitis Bart said: "I figured you for some kind of meditation type ... from Calcutta or Bombay."

Imitating an upper-class English accent, Arvanitis said: "Close, devilishly close, Brahms old chap!" Then, reverting to natural speech, he continued: "Actually, I'm a Buddhist monk but this is my day off so I'm passing as a Pennsylvania Greek." Leaning over toward Bart, Arvanitis spoke confidentially: "You've read my book, of course ... 'Zen And The Art of Used-Car Salesmanship?'"

"I'm afraid not," Bart said apologetically, going along with Arvanitis. "Are you really into Zen?"

"No, man, but I'm really into used cars. I sell 'em. Got my own lot back in Pittsburgh. Right now I'm on a bit of a sabbatical, so my kid brother George runs

the place for me. No doubt you've heard of my establishment – 'Oedipus Wrecks?'"

"You're a comedy writer, right?" Bart asked, still
uncertain about Arvanitis.

"So help me," Arvanitis answered, crossing his heart.
"Used cars."

Bart grinned. "Holy shit!" he said softly. They
struck him as an odd pair. The girl, even though she
sat in the shadow of an awning, shone. Everything
about her was orderly, and yet natural. Arvanitis, on
the other hand, looked as if he'd been spilled only
half-prepared from an electric mixer. Somehow there
was something forced and unnatural about his breezy
manner. "You two staying near here?" Bart asked.

"We're not ... together," Kathy O'Hearn replied.
She smiled, forgiving Bart for drawing yet another
wrong conclusion.

"We're at the same school," Arvanitis said. Bart
looked puzzled. Perceiving this, Arvanitis explained:
"Kathy and I are at the Summer Academy in Nice.
She's taking French. Believe it or not, yours truly is at
the Music Faculty taking a six-week course in Com-
position."

'You mean you're a musician?' Bart was impressed.
Arvanitis listed his accomplishments: a bachelor's
degree in musicology from Penn State, after college a
short stint as a percussionist with a big band, then a
small combo of his own. "It all started when I won a
songwriting contest sponsored by K D K A, Pittsburgh.
I was just a punk teenager then. Now I really want to
get down to some serious composing."

The obvious question was: how come the used car
business?

"Well, Brahms, that's a short story,' Arvanitis said.
The readiness with which he launched into it indi-
cated to Bart that, long or short, it was a well-rehearsed
story told often and with a certain amount of relish.
"You see," Arvanitis went on, "there comes a wonder-
fully insightful moment in the music business – it's like

a brain hemorrhage, it strikes without warning – maybe you're in the middle of playing your big solo in a club and some slob at a front table starts giving a waiter shit because he ordered his martini with vodka, not gin. Or suddenly the face you're shaving doesn't look like the fresh-faced kid in your eight-by-ten glossies. And you know ... boy, how you know! ... that you ain't gonna make it any further as a performer. You've blown it, lost the breaks. Poof!" Arvanitis laughed suddenly. "Know what I mean, Brahms?" He laughed again.

Bart didn't want to know what Arvanitis meant. He felt uneasy and cursed himself for having sat at this table. There was something false about Arvanitis' laughter, a quality of barely-suppressed hysteria; it was the laughter of a man pleading with the world to review the injustice of his ruined aspirations and to award him a generous judgment of pity. Notwithstanding the salad and lemonade which had arrived as Arvanitis spoke, Bart felt an urge to jump up and run from the restaurant. He wanted no more of this man's laugh-drenched recitation of failure.

Bart decided to take the initiative and say something positive. "I'm a musician too. I play sax in a rock band. As a matter of fact, just before I left Toronto we finished our first demonstration tape. Our producer sent them to a friend of his at Warner's. If they like our sound, we stand a good chance of getting a recording contract."

Arvanitis shook his head wisely. "I know ... I've done that whole lousy trip myself, kid." Again a self-pitying laugh that made Bart cringe. I don't want to hear about your whole lousy trip, Bart thought. But no, Arvanitis was determined to give the youngster from Toronto the benefit of his own bitter experience. On and on he went about his own attempts to inflate a more recent song into a hit single – getting as far as an audition with an influential disc jockey in New York, then the crushing verdict: too "cerebral" for the A.M. audience, not "commercial" enough; then watching the record become relegated to an early morning F.M. show where it died after two or three weeks of sporadic exposure. Arvanitis punctuated almost every sentence in the story of his demise with that quick nervous laugh. The lettuce in Bart's salad began to taste like tinfoil; in his mind he ran a large black "X" across this meal, the one bad meal he'd eaten thus far in his travels. Perhaps, he hoped, Kathy could reverse the downward trend. "What kind of French are you studying?" he asked her.

"French literature after World War II ... Camus, Sartre, de Beauvoir. I'm working on my Master's."

"Sounds heavy, doesn't it?" Arvanitis interrupted. "But Kathy's smart. She's gonna make it. She's not crazy like you and me, kid."

Bart resented the category into which Arvanitis had just lumped him. The nerve of this creep, Bart thought. Putting down his fork and looking coolly at Arvanitis, he said: "I don't think of myself as insane, you know."

Arvanitis scoffed. "Listen kid, rock bands are like rocks – a dime a dozen. Take a little advice from me. I've got no axe to grind, I can be completely objective about this, right? Just don't get your hopes up, that's all I can tell you."

Bart could feel his temper rising. "Do you automatically assume everybody you talk to is a born loser?" he asked. He was about to add "like you," but caught himself in time. It really didn't matter a damn to Bart at this point that he might inflict this touch of cruelty on the man next to him; what concerned him was how even an offhand slur would affect his image in Kathy O'Hearn's sight. Bart wasn't sure yet why it mattered to him, but it did.

Arvanitis pressed on. "Look kid, don't get uptight. I mean, don't ruin your vacation over this, for Chrisake. I'm just trying to get you to see —"

"Maybe he doesn't want to see," Kathy protested.

Arvanitis' expression instantly became petulant.

126

"Butt out, Katherine," he said. "You may be a whiz at French but you know bugger-all about this subject, baby."

"I paid for my own lunch, so you butt out," Kathy shot back at him. Flushed with anger, she glared at Arvanitis, defying him to order her out of the conversation.

Embarrassed, Arvanitis sat back. "Broads," he mumbled.

Turning to Bart, Kathy spoke up again. "I'm sorry about all this ... I really am."

"It's okay," Bart assured her. "Don't worry, everything's cool, honest."

Bart was beginning to like Kathy O'Hearn a great deal, much more than he wanted to like her. After all, there were so many other items on the agenda of his life ... priorities that needed his full attention.

At the age of nineteen going on twenty Bart Brahms had: (a) changed his name from Kevin to Bart, "Kevin" being somehow wrong for a potential pop music shaker and mover. "Bart" was cool; besides "Bart Brahms" had nice alliteration; (b) learned everything his teacher could teach him about playing the saxophone but talented as he was on the instrument, decided he'd rather be a maker (and breaker) of rock bands than play in them; (c) fallen in and out of love with an eighteen-year-old from Forest Hill (right side of the tracks) named Karen Frummer who was all screwed up because her idea of a terrific Saturday afternoon was a tour through the casual clothes section at Holt Renfrew; (d) fallen in and out of love with another eighteen-year-old from Bathurst Heights (wrong side of the tracks) named Sherry Bleckman who was all screwed up because her mother ran a hairdressing shop and her father ran a car wash, and neither parent understood their daughter's penchant for wearing Kodiak boots and writing poems about death, and in fact the whole Bleckman family was screwed up; and

127

(e) spent his seventeenth and eighteenth summers travelling down east and out west respectively after his sixteenth summer convinced him once and for all that Camp as an institution – including peeing off cabin porches at night, kitchen duty, seven-day canoe trips, and Visitors' Day – was for sucks.

So much for curricular activities.

Extra-curricularly young Brahms had smoked his way through first year of General Arts at University College and decided he'd had enough of academe. In spite of the dense nicotinous pall that constantly separated his eyes from the printed page, he'd managed to absorb enough Political Science to resolve that, if he didn't make it big in the music industry, he might go back to college someday and prepare himself to become Canada's first true Machiavellian. This secondary ambition was largely inspired by his poli-sci professor, an obnoxious ill-kempt New Yorker named Blumenthal who stank of cigars, needled his students mercilessly, and gave Brahms his only A-plus of that academic year, for an essay entitled "Against Institutionalism – The Way To The Good Life." In a frenetic hand Blumenthal scrawled across the last page: "Hail kindred soul!"

What else? Well, Bart Brahms had memorized enough rock song lyrics that, like the legendary Scheherazade, he could have recited for a 1,001 nights if the sparing of his life depended on it.

Moreover, at nineteen going on twenty, from seeds planted – often unwittingly – by Hershy and Louis Brahms, Bart had cultivated an orchard of ripe cynicism that shed its prickly vegetation upon all forms of human activity.

Accordingly, to Bart's way of thinking, it made no difference who the hell won the U.S. presidential election in November; all politicians were closet assholes. They came out of the closet the minute they started playing the Oval Room.

The constabulary was the final resort of the illiterate, a quasi-criminal army whose sleazy mission was to seek out Youthful Innocence wherever it could be found and give it a short sensible haircut.

For religion – "organized" religion – Bart reserved a special stockpile of contempt, damning all of it regardless of creed. Any form of supplication that began with bowed head and closed eyes and ended with "Amen" was to him laughable. Nor was he captivated by Oriental mysticism, especially such Oriental mysticism as could be found in the streets of Toronto. Saturday after Saturday the Hare Krishna types, beating their tom-toms and ding-ding-dinging their finger-cymbals would accost him on the sidewalk in front of Sam's Record Bar and invite him to examine the emptiness in his soul, unaware that at the entrance to Bart Brahms' spiritual lodgings there was posted in bold letters: "No Vacancies." As far as Bart Brahms was concerned, he was full up to here with the incorporeal ideas of the world.

Not that Bart Brahms was Godless, mind you. On the contrary, the fact was Bart Brahms loved God. He not only loved Him, he *liked* Him ... which nowadays meant a helluva lot more. Anybody could love. Liking ... that was deeper.

To be specific, Bart liked God's way of thinking. Take for instance motorbikes. If God had intended two-cylinder Yamahas to suffice, He wouldn't have created four-cylinder B.M.W.'s. If God in His divine wisdom had considered Selmer-Six saxophones the ultimate, He wouldn't have inspired the Selmer-Seven. It was God who, having perceived the rather humdrum limitations of ordinary tobacco, declared: "Let there be Pot!" And lo, there was Pot! It was God who, having invented the decibel, exhorted man to go forth and amplify!

Say what you would about a lot of the crap on this earth, one thing you had to admit: God was the God of bigger and better technology and broader horizons of pleasure. Life ... life was an Autobahn, twelve lanes, limited access, unlimited speed.

But somewhere in the mass of cylinders and twin exhausts and five-speed manual shifts and woofers and tweeters and pre-amps and jeans elegantly worn and torn and quality grass and the great glorious freedom to stare at tits and yell bullshit and refer to presidents as assholes and teachers as pricks ... somewhere in that diamond-bright diamond-hard kaleidoscope floated a lightbeam of ambition to be a man – to be more than a man – to be a Somebody.

Europe was intended to reopen all the fresh air vents of Bart's mind – vents he felt had come perilously close to being shut for all time in the droning dullness of university lecture halls. He would spend a couple of months in Europe, then return to Toronto in August and plunge with renewed vigour into the ear-splitting head-throbbing life of a would-be rock star. The following spring ... well, who knew? Maybe the big guns in California would sign his band for a tour, complete with a gig on the *Midnight Special* and even a guest appearance with Johnny Carson. Daydreams? Pie in the sky? Sure. But nowhere in the wide world was there an art form – or a business – or whatever you chose to call it – where the boundary between fantasy and reality was so invisible. Pie in the sky was the daily special of rock musicians; they thrived on it, grew fat on it. Later on, say in two or three years, with enough super-stardom tucked away in his ego to last two life-times and enough bread in the bank to finance a private militia of assorted flunkies, Bart could bid fare-well to the recording studio with its dense undergrowth of cables and wires and its microphone booms coming at him from every conceivable angle, and take the magic elevator ride upstairs to the big beige boardroom.

For the moment, however, one item of entirely un-related business took precedence over everything else: Kathy O'Hearn.

How weird, he thought; half an hour ago she didn't so much as exist in his life, and now nothing seemed to matter except proving to this stranger from Boston that he was not some damp-nosed little punk whom mommy and daddy had packed off to Europe for the summer because the choice facing them was either that or finding a niche for him in some obscure department of the family business. He felt more than drawn to Kathy; he was captivated by her. Well, being captivated was nothing new to the young man. During Bart's pimplehood, there had been all sorts of ardent panty probings with all sorts of girls. More recently, in his clear-skinned period, there had been deeper passion plays with Karen Frummer and Sherry Bleckman. Yet in their cases, when all was said and done, it hadn't mattered a damn to him. After all, what the hell was *their* long-range potential? Karen Frummer would probably end up some day living in cashmere comfort, married to a nice young doctor who was screwing his nurse on the side; Sherry would end up living on brown rice and natural bran, regularity her only claim to fame. But Kathy O'Hearn ... here was a different story. She was older for one thing; for another, she possessed a kind of unruffled beauty that was novel in Bart's experience.

Still, having to tolerate Arvanitis was a higher price than Bart Brahms was willing to pay for the pleasure of another few minutes of Kathy O'Hearn's company. From his rear pocket he withdrew a ten-franc note and slapped it on the table. "I hate to break this up folks," he said, "but I've got a date with a motorbike. Thanks for the education, Norman." Bart deliberately avoided a sarcastic tone and his expression of gratitude therefore sounded twice as sarcastic to Arvanitis.

"You'll learn kid, you'll learn," Arvanitis responded, with an air of fatality that was sickening to Bart.

To Kathy O'Hearn, Bart said: "So long. I hope we run into each other sometime."

She looked up at him. Her eyes were sad, compassionate. "So long," she said.

Bart grabbed up his shoulderbag and strode along the terrace and up a flight of flagstone steps – taking them two at a time – that led to a narrow street at the top of the cliff. By now the sun had accomplished its maximum objective for the day; heat radiated from two directions – the sun and the centre of the earth. Bart's jeans stuck to his behind and felt as if they were bonded to his crotch. He hoped to have a quick swim after lunch, but now his only aim was to mount his rented motorbike and get back to Beaulieu as quickly as possible. He'd found a small hotel on the eastern outskirts of town, not too far from Eze. It wasn't much, but it was cheap, clean, and there was a bath. Anyway, there certainly wasn't room that afternoon at St. Jean Cap Ferrat for both Bart Brahms and Norman Arvanitis.

He'd parked the motorbike under a small tree before going down to the terrace restaurant, but the sun had moved sufficiently to erase what little shade the tree could yield. As a result, the black motorcycle saddle was barely touchable. Bart straddled the seat and gingerly lowered his backside onto it. "Chee-rist!" he shouted. A passing pedestrian, attracted by the shout, turned, gazed at the young motorcyclist dispassionately, then shrugged. Bart shrugged back. "Shrugged ya last!" Bart called to the pedestrian. The pedestrian shrugged again, and walked on.

He was about to slam down the starter pedal when he heard his name called. He released his foot from the pedal and peered through his aviator sunglasses in the direction of the flagstone steps. "Bart ... wait a moment." It was Kathy O'Hearn.

She walked briskly toward him. "Just a sec, Bart —' She came within a pace or two of the motorcycle, then stopped. "Bart, I was wondering ... I forgot to ask you where you're staying."

"Just east of Beaulieu. Near Eze-sur-Mer."

Kathy looked disappointed.

"Did I say the wrong thing again?"

She smiled. "No, not really."

"You want a lift to Nice?"

"Thanks, but that's the exact opposite direction. It's a helluva distance out of your way. I can get a bus in the village. Besides, the traffic in Nice is incredible."

"I know ..." Bart paused. "I'm afraid I don't carry a spare helmet."

"I didn't expect you would," Kathy said.

"But I'll drive real careful."

They were in Nice in half an hour. By late afternoon, in Kathy's rented room in the hilly Cimiez district north of the city, Bart and Kathy lay in each other's arms on her bed, oblivious to the dead-still air in the place, to the constant screech of French tires coming through the open window from the hot pavement outside. As he gently explored with his fingers the peaceful contours of her face, a thought crossed Bart's mind: Kathy O'Hearn was the girl on his yacht. Kathy O'Hearn, and the yacht with the navy blue hull, and the helicopter roosting on the afterdeck ... Henri the steward fetching drinks ... and – don't forget, don't ever forget! – L.A. calling on the ship-to-shore.

After the sun had set they went to the beach and sat watching the sky and the sea merge into a solid dark blue curtain.

"I'm sorry about what happened with Norm Arvanitis today," Kathy said quietly.

"I don't want to talk about Norm Arvanitis."

"Does it upset you?"

"The only thing that upsets me is the thought of you spending time with a creep like that."

"He's not always a creep, Bart. Sometimes he's a very interesting person."

Bart chortled sardonically. "Interesting is a non-word."

"You sound like you've been to a shrink."

"I haven't, but my mother was into some kind of group thing for a while. I got that from her. One of the things she says she's learned is using words like 'lousy' or 'terrific,' but never 'interesting.' I remember one night my folks had a whole bunch of company for a buffet supper and they all started talking about education. Everybody was bitching like hell ... you know the kind of thing: somebody's kid's fifteen and can't write, somebody else's kid's seventeen and can't spell, the system's too lax, too liberal ... everybody shovelling shit at the schoolboards and the teachers. And all of a sudden ole Charlotte – that's my mother – comes lunging out of the jungle like a goddamn tiger. She must've bit the ass off everybody in the room. 'What're *you* personally doing about it? When's the last time *you* ever sat in on a Board of Education meeting? I bet *you* don't even know the name of your kid's math teacher ...' Things like that. The party sure died fast. I remember, as everybody was leaving, one of the men said: 'Thanks Charlotte, it's been an interesting evening.' You know what Charlotte did? Charlotte smiled sweetly at him and said: 'You're fulla shit, Lenny.' "

"Who's Lenny?"

"Lenny Winston. A close buddy of my dad's. *Was* a close buddy. After that, my folks didn't see too much of the Winstons."

"What did your father say at the time?"

"As far as I could tell, not a word. Not then, or afterward. Which really wasn't like him. He could be sarcastic as hell when he wanted to be. I'm not sure ... but I think he was seeing a shrink too. Maybe the same shrink as my mother."

"I think I'd like Charlotte," said Kathy.

Bart paused to reflect on this. Thoughtfully he said: "Not necessarily, Kathy. She isn't exactly mellowing in her old age. She's kinda tough to live with at times."

"How old is she?"

"In her mid-forties."

"That's not old, Bart."

"It seems old when you're going on twenty. God, I can't imagine what it'll be like to be in my forties. Or even in my thirties. How old're you, Kathy?"

"Twenty-three ... next birthday."

Bart laughed. "Hey," he said, "I'm having an affair with an older woman!"

"How 'bout that, folks!" Kathy said. They kissed. Kathy asked: "What's she so tough about, Bart?"

"Oh, mostly about me. She's on my back a fair amount. So's my father."

"You mean you still don't put your socks in the laundry?"

"We're way past the 'pick-up-your-underwear' stage. We're into the heavy stuff now. Career. Making a living. Being a true-blue Jew."

Kathy giggled. "I didn't know you were Jewish, Bart."

"Bullshit you didn't."

"Honest! I mean, Brahms . . . well I thought maybe you were German or Austrian."

"Our name was originally Abramsky, and we're Jewish as hell."

"But, you really don't —" Kathy halted the observation there.

Bart lay back on the gravelly beach and laughed. "You were really gonna come out with it, weren't you?"

"Okay, Bart. You really don't look Jewish. There. Said. Now do I go to hell, or does it happen later?"

Bart pulled her gently down toward him. "If you go to hell, baby, we go together."

"That sounded like Humphrey Bogart," she said.

"Wrong. Woody Allen."

A couple of days later Bart found a room in Cimiez within a mile of Kathy's. The run along the Corniche between Nice and Beaulieu had gotten much too long and, with the unrelenting heatwave and the desperation on the roadways, much too dangerous, even for a motorcyclist of Bart Brahms' daring and expertise. Kathy's classes took up the mornings. Afterward they lunched on pain-bagnats which were tasty, filling, and cheap, and chain-smoked Gauloises. In the evenings they ate couscous or souvlaki at tiny restaurants in old

135

Nice, and strolled among the crowds along the Promenade-des-Anglais. Late at night they would end up at Pub Valrose, a student hangout near the Academy where they drank brown beer and shared a slice of pizza.

In Kathy's room, or Bart's, they made love, and sat up, sometimes until dawn, telling each other their life stories and speculating about the future.

Kathy's father was Brendan O'Hearn II (Bick for short), son of Brendan O'Hearn I who had founded the famous O'Hearn Orthopaedic Clinic in Boston. After his wife had died giving birth to the last of their offspring, Bick O'Hearn had raised Kathy and five other children almost singlehandedly.

"He must have a very strong personality," Bart said.

"Strong, yes. He's also a very devout Catholic. I'm afraid I've been a bit of a disappointment to him in that respect. I'm not much of a churchgoer."

"Do you ever go to confession?"

"Occasionally. Why?"

"You gonna tell your friendly neighbourhood priest about you and me, babe?"

Kathy grinned: "I'm gonna blow his mind!" she said. Then she turned serious. "How do you think your parents would feel if they knew that their little true-blue Jew was having a mad passionate affair with Paddy McGinty's daughter?"

"What's it matter?" Bart said, testily. "I mean, it's a little late for me to go on playing the role of mommy-and-daddy's boy."

"None of us ever stops being somebody's child ... ever," Kathy said with an air of gentle resignation. "You can't just slice away certain complexities – like differences in religious background – and pretend they don't exist."

Bart fixed her with an earnest gaze. "Look Kathy, right now there are only two things that occupy my mind ... you, and making it big in music. Nothing else matters at the moment."

136

"But you can't shut your eyes to everything and everybody else."

"Why not?" Bart demanded. "Take your own father, Kathy; he must have kept his eye on one goal – medicine – and nothing else. I suppose that's okay, but the pop music industry isn't?"

"My father's first love was medicine, that's true. But at college he was into all sorts of things – track, the debating team—"

"Christ, Kathy, you really expect me to dress like Pat Boone and own season's tickets for the football games? Anyway, I bet the great Dr. O'Hearn outgrew all that crap, right?"

"Wrong. As a matter of fact he's chairman of a citizens' committee that's trying to stop supersonic jets from using Boston Airport. He's also on the Mayor's panel trying to work out the busing problem in Boston schools. Talk about sticking your neck out on issues!"

Bart snickered. "And after he's had it chopped a few times, where do you think it'll get him, Kathy? Somebody in Washington will get together with somebody in Paris or London and vroom! Look what's comin' down the Boston runway ... a Supersonic Jet. As for busing, Jesus Christ Himself wouldn't touch that one with a ten-foot pole. He's too smart."

"In other words, you believe in doing nothing about anything?" Kathy asked.

"I'm pissed off with that 'citizens' scene, Kathy. I had a bellyful of it when I was a teenie. None of the 'great causes' we made so much noise about ever got resolved ... I mean really resolved. The world just goes on getting more fucked up by the hour."

"What about your folks? Do they ever get ... involved?" Kathy pronounced "involved" as if the word had a significance far beyond its modest place in the dictionary. In the O'Hearn tradition, "getting involved" was a religion in itself. It meant being a card-carrying Democrat, raising funds for Catholic charities, being on the Symphony Board; of late, it also meant

137

getting out of the boardrooms and drawingrooms and into the streets and squares where the atmosphere crackled with dissent.

Grasping the importance Kathy attached to involvement, Bart replied, imitating her pronunciation: "Yes, my folks do get ... involved. There was a time when they – my father especially – couldn't have cared less about what went on. The world was something you saw for fifteen minutes on the eleven o'clock news. Then, at around the time of my bar mitzvah, when I was thirteen, things changed, *really* changed ..."

The impetus for change had come from the synagogue crisis.

For Charlotte Brahms there was a very personal and ironic dimension to that conflict. Having spent years attempting, without success, to press her husband into service at the temple, she was then faced with the desperate urge to *un*press him when the cause he was hired to espouse turned out to be in direct opposition to her own. But Hershy, thoroughly hooked by the new challenge in his life, was beyond disengagement. Charlotte could not bring herself to abandon her friend Rachel Mannheim, nor of course could she erase the fact that it was she who had written the report which fuelled the conflagration.

Hershy attributed Charlotte's intransigence to the twin inspirations of Rachel Mannheim and women's lib. "This is your new role as ball-breaker, isn't it Charlotte?" he said with a strong note of contempt in his voice.

Charlotte was equally uncomplimentary. "At least for me it's a new role. As for you, Hershy, there's nothing the least bit intellectual about your identification with Shulman and Roher," she said. 'This is just Hershel Brahms, doing what comes naturally to men ... the Male Hunter shtick."

The only practical solution was to go their separate ways on this issue. Neither was prepared to make the kind of sacrifices or compromises which, in former times, were blindly upheld as tokens of love, honour, obedience.

Only a last-minute settlement between Mrs. Mannheim and the rabbis prevented the cables of Charlotte and Hershy's marriage from snapping.

To Hershy Brahms went much of the credit for defusing the temple schism and keeping the battle out of the law courts after long months of negotiation. The catalyst was Brahms' agreement with Hollenberg, almost from the outset, that Samuel Cooperman's legal notions and archaic draftsmanship were more appropriate to Victorian times. It made more sense, Hershy reasoned, to negotiate new agreements from scratch. To Shulman and Roher he said: "In the long run you'll not only do yourselves a favour, you'll benefit your successors." Reluctantly the rabbis concurred, provided the pro-Mannheim forces would publish a retraction of certain statements previously published in the *Canadian Jewish Times*, and provided further that they – the rabbis – were permitted to use their own discretion at all times in questions of public protest.

"So long as such exercise of discretion is reasonable and does not reflect any discredit upon the temple," Mrs. Mannheim stipulated.

Agreed.

Brahms and Hollenberg together composed the statement of retraction for the press. And as for salary increases, a new point system was worked out based upon Mrs. Mannheim's beloved cost-of-living index and the rabbis' equally beloved concept of tenure. Minutes of settlement were signed, afterward there were stiff formal handshakes, and the principals, accompanied by their seconds, retired to their respective corners to gloat quietly over the concessions they had won and to cauterize their wounds.

For Charlotte and Hershy it was now impossible to restore their home life to the insulated cocoon it had once been.

Hershy found himself more sought after as a nego-tiator and arbitrator. His name began to appear on letterheads as a director of this organization and an advisor to that. More and more of his time was taken up with evening committee meetings and, to Louis' dismay, Sunday morning breakfast meetings. He no longer looked upon himself as a razorblade. Instead, he felt a new sense of power, a feeling of control over every new experience that came within his grasp.

Charlotte too came to recognize a new sense of power. Having insisted upon her right to stand at Rachel Mannheim's side and the hell with marital oaths, she was hardly eligible to revert to a daytime life that centred around gardening tools and household cleaners, and a nightlife that was a mixture of expen-sive diversion (dinner at *Chez Tony*) and inexpensive boredom (television). At one time it had irritated Charlotte no end that, as she and her contemporaries tiptoed warily out of their mid-thirties, the inevitable opening cross-examination at any meeting of two women was: "So what are you doing with yourself these days?" It was an out-and-out summons to render an account. Failure to answer satisfactorily brought swift and stern judgment from the interrogator. ("I find you, Charlotte Brahms, guilty of Gross Inactivity and sentence you to six months without 'Edge of Night.'") And yet now, in the post-crisis weeks, she was casting about, like an angler, in search of some scrappy ideological muskellunge that would tax her energies and intuition.

In the Ethic of Female Busyness, there was an hier-archical order of occupations: at the head of the list was the pursuit of a doctorate, perhaps in social work or clinical psychology; then followed degrees in the humanities (a little selfish perhaps but nevertheless enriching); then, down the line a bit, public relations, the opening of a boutique for the sale of imported goodies in a "high ticket" shopping district, art or cooking classes. Perusing the syllabus, Charlotte decided none of these was for her. But what to do? After all, she told herself, one must not sit upon one's ass waiting for menopause. No indeed, one must proceed into the Big Evening of one's life, both in mind and body, with nothing less than racquet-swinging rage.

For Charlotte Brahms, politics – specifically the politics of education – became the answer to "What are you doing with yourself these days?"

All the incentives were present: Bart's loud and bitter dissatisfaction with his high school – a gigantic mill where the prime concern was keeping order in the halls between classes; a curriculum that was in reality a batch of untested recipes for learning issued from time to time by the Education Ministry's chefs; and an entrenched trustee in Brahms' ward who had squeezed a lot of political mileage out of his degree in Education but was finally beginning to lose credibility with the voters. Finding this field of political action readily accessible to neophyte activists, Charlotte went about recruiting citizens into a newly-formed Parents' Association whose aims was to gain direct decision-making power in all aspects of education. Within a year she was known as the scourge of the secondary schools. Within another year she was president of the Parents' Association. After two terms in that office she took on the incumbent trustee at the polls. She lost – but by a paper-thin margin that left her champing for a re-match.

Bart had witnessed most of these parental transformations from the sidelines, preferring to remain detached except during the occasional dinnertable debate when he would offer gratuitous advice to Hershy ("I'd tell both sides to kiss off if I were you") and to Charlotte ("You're wasting your time; the whole Board are idiots!"). Oh sure, he admitted, it was far out being escorted to your table at Cy's Rib 'n Bib by the owner himself, having him wink at you and say: "So you're Mr. Brahms' boy eh? Well, I hope you turn out like your Dad." And it wasn't hard to take when the

141

head of the English department at school whispered in your ear: "Wish your mother good luck for me ... she's got a lot of guts."

Relating these events and feelings to Kathy, Bart said: "You could say that my parents are really Somebodies now. Trouble is, being that kind of a Somebody doesn't seem like much fun. It's all work, no play. The price tag is too damn high."

"But that's what being involved is all about," Kathy contended.

"Oh God," Bart cried, "there's that word again."

"Okay," Kathy said hastily, "forget I said 'involved.' Call it Social Consciousness, then. How does that grab you? After all, social consciousness is what the folk and rock scene is really all about."

Bart sighed, exasperated. "God, Kathy, where have you been hiding? What makes you think pop music has anything to do with social consciousness? Do you know what pop music is all about today ... I'm not talking about 1965 or 1970 ... but *today*? It's all about entertainment, pure and simple. While all the cats and chicks with the gee-tahrs and the hobo hats are up there on the stage bullshitting the audience about free love and how clean the water used to be before there was plumbing, the cats and chicks in the back office are keeping an eye on the charts and kissing-ass with the disc jockeys and hyping and hyping and hyping like crazy. That's what the business is about. Forget Chicago in '68, and Woodstock and all that shit. Anyway, the truth is, it was just as phony back then, too."

"If it's so phony, why would you want any part of it?"

Bart's face lit up. "Because it's exciting as hell, Kathy! The critics can bitch all they like about limited chord changes and banal lyrics but the fact is, there isn't a field of entertainment that's got that terrific feeling of spontaneity you find in rock. Besides, culture doesn't always mean laying heavy trips on the audience. Look at Mozart for instance. The local prince would call him up and say: 'Listen Wolfgang, I've got three hundred coming for dinner Saturday night and I need a coupla dozen yards of dinner music ... by the way, we're serving chicken,' and presto! – chicken music for three hundred. You didn't catch Mozart writing protest songs about how lousy it was to be broke or suffering from a dose of clap."

"Mozart's music is still being played and he's been dead nearly two hundred years. Do you honestly think any of that pop stuff will be played a couple of hundred years from now, Bart? Even the Beatles and Stones?"

"I don't give a damn. I'm not going to be alive two centuries from now, obviously. If I write a song for our band I don't say to myself: Now let me see, is this going to be immortal? Is this a masterpiece? Those are judgments other people have to make later. Often much later."

"You make it all sound so fleeting and accidental," Kathy said. "The trouble with you is that you have no sense of history or posterity."

"Kathy, I've heard that old line about people who ignore history being doomed to relive it, and frankly I think it's a clever line but really a crock of shit. Show me two historians who can get together and agree on a single version of past events. As for posterity, people who live with their eyes glued to the future give me a pain in the ass; they have no talent for enjoying the present. They even screw with one eye on the clock and the other on the calendar. No, posterity's a crock of shit too, as far as I'm concerned."

Kathy looked perplexed. "But I thought it's a particular crock Jews live by," she said. "One of my father's associates, Dr. Grossberg, has a motto framed on the wall of his office that reads: 'Why am I sitting when I could be standing, standing when I could be walking, walking when I could be running?'"

"That may be a terrific slogan to put up in an orthopedic clinic to inspire the customers, but it's a lousy code for a man with healthy bones. Let me tell you something Kathy: I want all of my options open all of the time. To me a man's dead when his options die, even if his organs are all functioning full blast."

Kathy studied Bart's face, watched his cheeks collapse inward against the facial bones as he drew deeply, intensely, on his cigarette. Full of affection, she said: "There's a sense of urgency about the way you smoke a cigarette, did you know that? It's like every draw is your last before they put the hood over your head and shoot you. Do you really think you'll last beyond whatever your vision is today?"

"Don't you think I will?" he asked.

"I wonder. There's this awful air of restlessness about you. You talk about others not having the talent or time to enjoy the present, but I'm not sure you've got it either. I mean, when you pluck yourself out of the past, and don't allow yourself to think about the long-range future, it seems to me you're left standing in a tiny circle ... like you've painted yourself into a corner somewhere out in space."

"I think the cliché you're searching for is 'Alienation,'" said Bart, with mock sobriety.

"You're making fun of me."

"No, God, I swear," he lied, frowning, certifying this to be true by holding up his right hand, then breaking into a grin.

"Yes you are." Kathy said this sadly, pensively, as if she had just had a vision of an unbreachable wall between the two of them. "You *are* making fun of me."

"I don't mean to, Kathy, honest. It's just that ... well, I've heard that alienation thing ever since I learned how to spell 'rock.'"

"It's true though, Bart. There's a kind of deep-rooted anger that seems to come out of the music and the words and everybody associated with it. The whole thing ... seems so ... so hostile all the time."

"Then how come? ..." Bart paused.

"How come what, Bart?"

"Never mind," he replied.

"How come what?" she repeated.

Bart looked away. "How come ... I'm staying in Nice ... as long as you're here?"

"Who says you are?"

"I say. I've decided."

"But you won't get to see Italy, or Greece, or —'

"Shut up, Kathy," he said lovingly. "You're ruining the first unhostile long-range plan I've ever made."

During the days and nights that followed, Kathy O'Hearn and Bart Brahms allowed nothing to come between them. Even the intense white heat of the Riviera sun couldn't separate them for more than the few minute they took each day to dash into the cooling turquoise of the Mediterranean.

Looking disgruntled, Bart Brahms emerged from the American Express office on the Promenade-des-Anglais and walked in the bright morning sun toward Kathy standing guard over the motorbike in a no-parking zone.

"Guess what?" he asked drily.

"You've been drafted."

"Worse than that, dummy," Bart replied. "Guess again."

"I give up."

He handed her a slip of paper. She read the brief message, then handed it back to him. "*Tonight?*" she asked. Bart nodded yes. "Here? In Nice?" Bart nodded again. "Did you have even a clue they were coming?" Kathy asked.

"No."

"What time will they be here?"

"I checked," Bart said. "The plane arrives at Nice Airport at 7:45."

"But I thought they were supposed to go straight back to Toronto from Tel Aviv."

"Well, I figure Charlotte's dropping in to check the laundry situation. Hershy's gonna ask me how the money situation is." Bart lowered his voice half an octave – "tell me, kid, how's the money situation?' Lou . . . well, Lou's where you come in, Kathy."

"Me?"

"Yeah, the family needs a blood sacrifice, and you're it. Once a year my grandfather consumes a little Irish Roman Catholic girl. It's a ritual the Jews used to perform back in his hometown in Russia. He's bonkers about the Boston-baked kind."

Bart's attempt at levity did little to dispel Kathy's apprehension, or his own for that matter. This turn of events had caught him completely by surprise and unprepared. Charlotte and Hershy had just ended two weeks' tour of Israel (their first) with Louis Brahms, who was making his second visit to that country. The package deal included a brief stop, both going and returning, at the airport in Paris. Obviously the temptation to visit Bart was too much for the trio; thus their decision to depart from the packaged arrangements and fly to Nice.

Kathy and Bart stood beside the motorbike, scowling.

"I'm scared, Bart," Kathy said.

Delivering a gentle fist to her chin, he said in his best Borgartese: "You're gonna get in there and knock 'em dead kid."

"No fooling, Bart, I mean it. I'm really scared."

"Bullshit."

"The thought of meeting your family in one swell foop . . . maybe, maybe it would be better if I quietly get lost for a few days . . . just while they're in Nice."

"Look Kathy, tonight you'll come to the airport —"

"No way!" Kathy interrupted. "Going to airports gives me terminal illness."

Bart stared at Kathy in disbelief. "You're really serious, aren't you?"

"You remember what I said about denying complexities."

"Godammit Kathy, there you go lecturing again."

"Godammit Bart, do you think I'm going to step up

146

to them at the airport and say howdy folks I've been sleeping with your son and my name's Kathy O'Hearn and I'm an R.C. and we're in love, did you have a pleasant flight?"

They struck a bargain: Bart would go alone to the airport that evening, spend the following morning and afternoon with them, tell them about Kathy; then, if all systems were go, Kathy would join them later for dinner.

What Bart had no way of knowing was that all systems had begun to come apart hours before. The trip from Tel Aviv to Paris was a botched affair – scrambled reservations, a super-efficient security officer at Tel Aviv explaining that the whole mess was really not the fault of the airline but was the result of whatever was going on at a place called Entebbe in Uganda, delayed departure, and late arrival at Paris. They missed the connection for the plane to Nice, and Charlotte, Hershy and Louis were obliged to spend Sunday in Paris. For relief from the heat more than anything else, they had taken an hour's ride on the Seine in a sightseeing boat only to disembark on a stifling platform full of Coke machines that didn't work. Somehow Hershy and Charlotte lost Louis in the throng in St. Germain des Près later in the afternoon and only by a miracle did they spot him seated in a sidewalk café drinking a beer, giving his complete attention to a young Parisian couple next to him busily exploring the insides of each other's mouths between sips of lemonade. After dinner (which cost Hershy an arm and a leg because the restaurant had air-conditioning) they lost Louis again – this time on the Champs Elysées. Another miracle: they found him near the eternal flame at the Arc de Triomphe talking sign-language and disjointed English to a gendarme. The gendarme was pointing to a small Star of David flag pinned to Louis' lapel and babbling something about Entebbe which nobody, except the Frenchman, understood. Finally, late that evening in Paris, Louis announced that, much as he would love to see his grandson and the Riviera, he preferred to stay over on his own in Paris for an extra day or two, then he'd join them in the south. To this announcement Hershy reacted by exploding and stomping off to his room. Charlotte sat in Louis' room pleading with her father-in-law to change his mind. Paris was no place to be alone – the heat, the crowds, the crazy drivers, the pickpockets ... Reluctantly Louis agreed to go on to Nice. At least he would have most of the following day to spend in Paris before they headed south to the Riviera.

On the plane bound for Nice, Hershy issued a stern directive to the others, which he took the trouble to repeat as the aircraft made its descent over the airport: "Now remember, don't keep bugging Bart about how he is. He's not a baby anymore."

"Hershy's right," Charlotte said to Louis.

"Don't worry, I understand perfectly," Louis agreed solemnly.

Before the reunion at Nice Airport was a minute old, Bart found himself pinned under a microscope.

"Let me look at you!" Louis kept repeating, unable to conceal his relief that his grandson hadn't starved, been kidnapped, or beaten to death and dumped in the sea. "Are you okay? Let me look at you!"

Charlotte peered at the collar of Bart's white (well, off-white) t-shirt, then fumbled in her overstuffed flight bag. "Take this, dear, it works miracles in cold water," she said, handing him a small packet of detergent.

"You want me to do my laundry right here, Mother?" Bart said straight-faced.

"Never mind that, for Chrisake," Louis exclaimed, "let me look at you! Are you okay?"

"Of course he's okay," Hershy interjected, smiling confidently. "Why shouldn't he be okay? He's not a baby." He threw an arm around Bart's neck. "Tell me honestly Bart," he said, suddenly turning serious, "is everything okay?"

148

"Everything's okay," Bart smiled. It was the first time any of them had given him an opportunity to answer.

While they waited for their luggage, Hershy stood close to Bart, resting one hand on his son's shoulder, slapping himself in the midsection with his free hand. "You know something, kid," Hershy said, "whenever you travel over here somebody's waiting to rip you off. I never go out without this." Again he slapped his middle where his moneybelt lay flat against his stomach, hidden under his creased cotton leisure suit. "A man gets very security conscious in his old age."

"That's terrific, Dad," Bart said, convinced his father was either suffering jet lag or going bananas.

The tourist bureau at the airport found them a hotel – the d'Albion – a modest establishment located on a side-street in the centre of Nice. Bart shepherded the others out of the terminal and into a cab. Thanks to a temporary lull in the traffic, the driver made it to the hotel without so much as a cross word to another motorist – a rarity in Nice. "Well," said Bart cheerfully, after the cabdriver unloaded the bags at the hotel entrance, "so far so good."

He'd spoken too soon.

"Christ, look at this." Hershy said. "This is all I need to see right now."

Below the polished brass plate bearing the hotel's name, a marble slab the size of a tombstone had been installed. They stood, baggage in hand, reading the inscription which was in French.

"What's it say?" Louis asked. "I see the word Gestapo."

Charlotte translated: "It says that two men, Raoul Bres and André Dujat, were arrested right in this hotel, one on January 5, 1944 and the other October 19, 1943; that both were interned at Schirmech, and executed September 1, 1944 by the Gestapo, and that they died for France and liberty, and that people should remember them."

"Bres? Dujat? Were they French Jews?" Louis wondered.

"It doesn't say. My guess is they were French French," said Charlotte.

Louis nodded his head dourly. "Sonofabitch Nazis."

Inside the hotel, the small lobby and the tiny bar adjoining teemed with a busload of middle-aged German tourists.

The Germans had arrived a few minutes earlier and were chattering animatedly as they sorted out their luggage and waited for their room keys to be distributed.

The night clerk was a small handsome man with white brushcut hair and a neatly trimmed military moustache. Fluent in German, he greeted Hershy with: "Guten Abend, Herr Brahms. Sie wollen zwei Zimmer, nicht wahr?"

"We're Canadians," Hershy said.

"I beg your pardon," the night clerk said, instantly switching to flawless English, "I assumed Brahms is German."

"God forbid," Louis muttered.

Their rooms faced boulevard Dubouchage. Hoping to entice a little fresh air into their rooms, they had thrown open the large old-fashioned windows as wide as possible, but the air merely squatted outside, heavy with the heat of the day just ending, awaiting the additional burden of heat (compounded with carbon monoxide) that was certain to arrive at sunrise. From somewhere in a neighbouring apartment block a man and woman were screaming at each other. Throughout the night motorbikes sped along the narrow dark boulevard with noisy urgency. From time to time the ugly sing-song of a police or ambulance alarm – "dee*dah*, dee*dah*, dee*dah*" – split the air, broadcasting the commission of yet another crime or the occurrence of yet another disaster in beautiful Nice. It was the same chilling two-note alarm Hershy remembered hearing in the closing moments of *Diary of Anne Frank* as

150

Anne waited helplessly for the police to break into her family's once-secret hideaway. Godalmighty, that sound should be legislated off the face of the earth, Hershy thought as he and Charlotte lay now atop the sheets, wilting in a hotel where once the Gestapo had pounded their gunbutts on doors and shouted "Raus ... schnell!" In the rooms along the corridor lay other tourists – ruddy-complexioned men and pink-skinned hausfraus from Deutschland, all in their forties and fifties, perspiration building on their bodies and evaporating into the sticky atmosphere of Nice. Half awake, half dreaming, Hershy heard a sharp rap on the door. They're here, he thought; they've found us ... Yes, yes the name's Brahms but we're Canadians ... My father? ... Yes, in the next room, but he's not really Jewish either, I mean we're *all* Canadians ... Look, here are our passports, see for yourself ... Well maybe I do look Jewish but that's only because I look like my mother and she looked Jewish but she was Canadian too godammit! She even worked for a member of parliament and didn't have a Jewish accent or anything like that, I swear! ... Wait a minute, listen to me, *listen*! ...

It was only when Hershy touched Charlotte's damp body that he knew for certain he was not on his way to Schirmech to join Raoul Bres and André Dujat in front of an S.S. firing squad.

Next morning Bart came down from Cimiez and they breakfasted together in the hotel diningroom.

"Is this all they ever give you to eat in the morning?" Louis asked, looking down at the regulation continental fare – croissants, thin pat of butter, cup of muddy café-au-lait.

"You can have mine if you're so hungry," Hershy said. "I have no appetite this morning. I must've been up the whole night."

"How come?" Bart asked. "Did the heat get you?"

"It wasn't really the heat," Hershy said. "It was those bloody awful ambulance and police sirens." Hershy imitated the sound. "It must be a sign of my basic insecurity. Each time I heard the sound of a heavy truck down in the street, or that dee*dah*, dee*dah*, I was sure it was the Gestapo coming to arrest *me!*"

At the word "Gestapo" a tourist at the next table turned and glanced at the Brahmses. He was tanned and wiry, in his late fifties perhaps. The three others at his table spoke German. The man returned to his conversation with his companions.

"Where were *you* in '42?" Hershy muttered under his breath.

"Hershy, for Godsake—" Charlotte whispered anxiously.

"What's with you, Dad?" Bart said. "I've never seen you paranoid like this before."

"I don't know – maybe I'm just overtired. We were on the go day and night in Israel. Even the couple of days' rest in Natanya at the end of the tour didn't help. I guess I'm still all wound up."

"You mean you've come away all gung-ho on Israel?" Bart asked.

"Yes ... and no. I don't know. There's so much to absorb, so much to think about. It seems like they throw forty centuries at you in two weeks. I'm not even sure I can sort out all of my feelings about the place. There's a kind of gnawing ambivalence."

Charlotte and Louis, on the other hand, were totally enthusiastic.

For Charlotte, the visits to the hospitals and forests and universities at last justified all the brownies she'd baked, the tickets she'd sold, the endless phone lists, committee meetings, rummage sales. An early riser, she was first into the breakfast room and onto the bus in the morning, and pressed as close to the Israeli tour guide as decency allowed, in order to catch every syllable of ancient and modern history that tumbled well-rehearsed from his lips. Teasing, Hershy said on the final day: "Charlotte, you forgot to ask him what octane gas the tour bus uses."

152

For Louis there was a reunion with the woman he'd met seven years ago – the one from Vancouver who had progressed from unhappy cashier in a hotel bar to happy divorcée with a small boutique of her own in Haifa. "I don't need all the sightseeing; go, go and don't worry about me, I'll be okay," Louis urged, pushing Hershy and Charlotte onto the long silver and blue bus. Louis, moreover, was greatly relieved to learn that his cousin Zvi (né Moishe) had gone to America ("Imagine not telling me!" Louis cried, grinning with delight) and had left Malka The Superman behind, apparently for good. Louis hadn't intended to look them up anyway, but at least now he didn't feel guilty. Louis Brahms had himself a fine time in Haifa. When the plane lifted off the runway at Tel Aviv, he wept a little.

"Well, ambivalent or not," Bart said to his father, "you must be turned on by this morning's news."

"What news?"

"You mean you haven't heard? The Israelis pulled off this fantastic raid on Entebbe yesterday ... rescued nearly all the people that were being held by the hijackers at the airport."

Charlotte lit up. "Of course ... that explains the policeman at the Arc de Triomphe —"

"I haven't seen today's *Herald Trib*," Bart said, "but it's page one in all the French papers. Knocked yesterday's U.S. Bicentennial story right into the want-ads."

Charlotte's countenance was beatific. "I don't know which news is more thrilling ... the rescue story, or the fact that you're into French newspapers," she said to Bart.

"I'm into a lot of things in France that I was never into before," Bart said.

"I'm going to pretend I didn't hear that remark," said Charlotte, playing martyr.

"Tell me, Bart," Hershy asked, "would you ever want to live in this country?"

"At the outset I thought: no, never," Bart said. "A lot of things turned me off, especially those first few days in Paris. But once I started down through the chateaux country and got into the Auvergne district and Aix-en-Provence it started to get to me. Now I guess I'm hooked. I've gotten to like a lot of things the French like."

"Really?" Hershy asked. "What do they like – besides American money?"

"Well, let me see ... the French like: carbon monoxide ... German shepherds – the dogs, not the men ... cardboard toiletpaper ... corners ..."

"Corners?"

"Uh huh. The things they turn on two wheels at the height of rush-hour traffic."

"What else?"

"Boobs," Bart continued. "Big boobs. Little boobs. Medium boobs. Any kind of boobs actually. Also pictures of boobs."

"I didn't know you were so infatuated with bosoms," Charlotte said.

"Infatuation has nothing to do with it," Bart protested. "Boobs are part of France's geography. They're as natural to the land as restaurants. This beach we swim at all the time – at St. Jean Cap Ferrat – it's a geographer's paradise."

To Hershy and Charlotte, Bart's description of St. Jean was amusing. But Louis Brahms was more than amused. "Tell me," he said to his grandson, "this beach you go to ... it's far from here?"

"About half an hour or so, by car."

Louis turned to Hershy. "Maybe we could rent a car? —"

While Hershy was occupied at the car rental office struggling through the fine French print of the lease, Bart disappeared long enough to find a public telephone and call Kathy. "It's not the best of times, Kathy," he said. "I mean, they're not getting any younger, and the heat and traffic and everything ... but as long as they don't come unglued anymore than they already have, I think the coast is clear for dinner."

"Have you told them about me, Bart?"

"No, not yet."

"Why not? What's wrong?"

"Nothing's wrong, honest. I'm just waiting for ... for a more suitable time. You know how it is, Kathy, they're feeling pretty unsettled ... kind of like going from one culture shock right into another."

"Then they don't know about your plans to stay in France past the summer, either?"

"Not yet."

"Have a nice dinner," Kathy said abruptly. "I'll see you tomorrow maybe."

"Kathy for Chrisake, listen to me. My folks aren't exactly Mr. and Mrs. Frankenstein. I tell you everything'll be okay. In fact, I think a few hours on the beach, and a swim, will make them feel like new. Meet us at St. Jean after your seminar. Can you catch the bus and get out there in time for a swim?"

"I don't know, Bart."

"Kathy, if the situation was reversed, I'd do it. I'd bust my ass to meet your family, and you goddamn well know it."

Kathy said nothing; she was perplexed. Was this the same Bart Brahms who, only a few days ago, purported not to give a damn any longer about parental ties? Nothing else mattered, Bart had told her, except his musical career and his relationship with her. Why then, this arm-twisting about meeting Hershy and Charlotte and Louis? Did young Mr Brahms' brassy exterior conceal, after all, a core of pure marshmallow?

"Kathy? Are you still there? Meet us at the beach. I'll keep an eye out for you. Anyway you won't have any trouble finding us. My dad'll be the only guy in the Mediterranean with a moneybelt tied around his bathing suit." There was silence still from the other end of the line. "Kathy?"

"Okay, okay," Kathy answered, "don't bug me, Bart. I'll see you there."

*

Treading gingerly over the tiny rocks that dug into the soles of his feet, Louis Brahms emerged from the water and made his way slowly up the beach to the umbrella they had rented.

"Feh!" he said. "Salt water. I feel like a herring."

"Since when don't you like salt water?" asked Hershy. "You swam in it in Israel."

"That was real salt. This stuff tastes like it's dumped out from a jar of pickles. Feh!"

"You're just looking for an excuse to park yourself under this umbrella for the rest of the day and stare at the neighbours," Bart said to Louis.

Louis dug a toe into Bart's stomach. "Okay smart aleck, off your tuchis and into the water, seeing you like it so much. I got important business here." Louis turned to Charlotte and Hershy. "That goes for you too. Go on. I'll look after everything."

"You'll keep an eye on everything?" Hershy said, not certain whether to trust the old man's powers of vigilance.

"I said I would, didn't I?"

"Well, I just want to be sure." Hershy began a routine check: "Moneybelt, passports ... Charlotte, where's your gold lighter?"

"Oh for Godsake, go already before they close the ocean for the night!" Louis blustered.

Hershy glared at his father. It was such a cinch to be old, or even young, he thought; there was no essential difference between the two; both seemed forever to be looking up, pleading "Carry me —" And Hershy Brahms was weary, so weary of all the lifting and carrying, that seemed to fall to his generation – the Generation In Between – the generation of redcaps. Truculently to Louis he said: "Somebody has to assume these responsibilities."

But Louis only brushed him off good-naturedly. "When we get back to Toronto I'll see to it you get a medal, my boy. Now stop being a pain in the ass and go take your wife for a swim."

Charlotte decided to swim out to a large raft a few hundred feet from the shore. "That's too strenuous for me," Hershy said. "I'll just stay close to the shore and float."

He stood watching Charlotte slide into the glistening water and soon lost sight of her as she became part of a sea of heads bobbing among the gentle wavecrests.

Surveying the crowds on the beach, he was able to pick out women here and there – some young, some not so young – sitting or lying topless under the sun, or beneath their umbrellas. Some of the women fussed impatiently with their young children, their matronly brows furrowed with a resentfulness that was not at all in harmony with the inviting softness of their bare bosoms. Others lay motionless, their thighs touching the thighs of their men, their hands flat on the sand at their sides, communicating only by the subtlest shifts of a finger or toe, as if they'd taken oaths of silence and inertia. Hershy imagined they were testing their abilities to disregard each other's bodies, but that any moment now their glands and bloodvessels would begin to boil and bubble and, upon an invisible, inaudible signal, they would suddenly fling themselves upon each other like starved carnivora.

Within his own glands and bloodvessels there was also a minute of boiling and bubbling, then it dwindled into a few seconds of velleity ... then nothing but calm curiosity.

Still scanning the beach, in water up to his chest, Hershy recognized Bart coming down the steps from the terrace restaurant accompanied by a girl. Taking her hand, Bart led her across the sand to the Brahms' umbrellad oasis where Louis Brahms sat like a security guard. He observed Louis rising and shaking the girl's hand. The three – Louis, the girl, Bart – seemed to plunge into animated conversation. "For Godsake," Hershy muttered, "don't take your eyes off my moneybelt. It's probably a trick to divert your attention. Who knows who the hell she is!"

Suddenly, from behind, Hershy felt a hand tugging at his trunks and a voice simultaneously yelled "Boo!" He swung round. "Charlotte! Jesus Christ —" She rose half out of the water and put her arms around his neck, letting her legs float upward behind her in the buoyant water.

"Charlotte, what the hell —"

He saw that her bra was tied around her middle and that her breasts hung free and white just beneath the water's surface.

"What the hell d'ya think you're doing?" he asked, looking around him in embarrassment.

"What the hell d'ya think I'm doing?" she replied, drawing her legs forward and locking them around his, forcing him off balance so that together they sank heavily to the bottom. Coming up, still somehow entwined, they shook the saltwater from their hair and opened their eyes.

"Hi!" It was Bart, in the water next to them. At his side stood the girl Hershy had seen a few minutes earlier. "This is Kathy ... Kathy O'Hearn."

"Oh my God!" said Charlotte Brahms. Her bra had disappeared.

On Bart's advice they took a table in the open air in one of the more remote corners of The African Queen where they could gaze at the crowds strolling along the quay, enjoy a fine view of Beaulieu's magnificent harbour and, with luck, escape the musicians and hawkers who wandered among the diners peddling poorly-played melodies and touristy aboriginal trinkets from Morocco and Algeria.

Earlier, during the drive into Beaulieu, and now over drinks at the restaurant, Bart's parents and grandfather kept up a lively though surface interrogation of Kathy O'Hearn, dipping occasionally into the subheadings of name, rank and serial number to inquire about her background in Boston, but demanding, and receiving in turn, little more than the normal yield produced by polite questions and answers. It was obvious that they liked Kathy. After all, what was there *not* to like? And it was equally obvious that they took her presence seriously on the reasonable assumption that Bart didn't go out of his way to invite her along just because he liked the way she ate. Still, Bart knew they were evaluating every tidbit of information the way intelligence officers analyze reconnaissance reports ... searching for even the tiniest outcroppings that could snag an innocent Jewish youth into premature husbandhood and, worse still, parenthood. Glancing at Louis, Bart detected by the rapt expression on the old man's face that he was studying the girl carefully. Occasionally, as she replied to a question, he would nod wisely. Louis always nodded wisely – and said nothing – whenever the news entering his ears brought mixed tidings.

The tabletalk turned to Entebbe. By now they had all read the day's issue of the *International Herald Tribune*, the front page of which was almost completely taken up with the rescue story.

"As lovely as it is here," Charlotte said, "I'm sorry we're not in Tel Aviv tonight. The atmosphere must be nothing short of delirious. What a shot in the arm for the Israelis!"

Bart smirked, as he did whenever the subject matter was political. "Today a shot in the arm. Tomorrow – a shot in the ass."

"Oh Bart," Charlotte hissed impatiently, "can't you leave your cynicism in the closet for one night?"

"Mother, let's face it, when all the hootin' and hollerin' are over and done with, Entebbe will not make so much as a pinch of shit's difference to Israel's position in the world."

"On the contrary, it was one of the noblest, most daring, exploits of this century."

"Tell that to the guy in Cornstalk, Saskatchewan when gas goes up to a buck a gallon."

"Bart, you don't seem to realize," Louis interjected,

"that it wasn't just Jews that were saved. There were others ... Frenchmen, Americans for instance."

Bart laughed. "Frenchmen! A month from now they won't even bother to make a cartoon out of the whole affair; they know what side their croissant is buttered on. Now the Americans ... that's different. By this time next week they'll have everything on the market from an album of Entebbe music to Entebbe t-shirts and breakfast cereal. And as for all the Jewish armchair hawks back home —"

"I think you've made your point, Bart," Hershy interrupted.

Bart was unaccustomed to having his freedom of speech pruned; he felt humiliated – all the more so because of Kathy's presence – and moved quickly to retaliate. "You really have freaked out on all the propaganda after all, haven't you, Dad?"

"There are aspects of Israeli life that have left me profoundly impressed, if that's what you mean."

Bart was not about to let up. "Profoundly impressed ... but still going home, right? Home to neat old Canada?"

"Okay, Bart ... so once again you're a genius at rooting out absurdities. I suppose you expect me to turn right around now and head back to Israel? Live in a kibbutz? Dig a ditch? Carry a gun? Well, if that's what you expect, I'm afraid you're in for a big disappointment, kiddo. Israel is a land of great wonders, but it's not for me. 'Neat old Canada' as you call it – that's for me. And don't get cute and try to instil some kind of shame in me for feeling the way I do. Some day you'll learn – no matter where a Jew lives on this earth, he faces a frontier."

"What frontier do you and your buddies on Richmond Street face?" Bart scoffed.

"It's me and my buddies on Richmond Street that keep you and your buddies on the beaches of Beaulieu," Hershy shot back. No sooner had this riposte escaped Hershy's lips than he realized that he had failed at a

160

crucial moment. He cursed himself and wished he could somehow scoop up his words and incinerate them in a sealed bag, like refuse. Too late, however; what was said was said.

Abruptly Bart rose from the table.

"Where are you going?" Charlotte asked anxiously. She had witnessed sudden exits like this before, knew they were Bart's way of bringing matters to a swift and uneasy finale whenever he felt parental clutches too tightly upon him.

"I'm out of cigarettes," Bart said.

Charlotte pointed to a box of cigarettes beside his plate. "There's still half a package —" she began. But Bart was already on his way.

"Bart?" Kathy called after him. "It's okay," he called back, without turning to look at her.

"Maybe you should go after him," Louis said to Hershy. He looked at Bart's untouched plate. "It's a shame," Louis said, "all that food."

Hershy, however, remained motionless. Angry with Bart, angrier with himself, he wondered why every discussion between the two of them in recent months promptly degenerated into a wrestling match where merely chalking up points was not enough, where the object was to score a complete fall in fifty words or less. He watched his son march with a determined agile step along the quay and disappear among the throngs of strollers, and although the thought was almost unbearable to him, Hershy wished he hadn't come to Nice. It seemed to Hershy Brahms that here – in the midst of all the gaily-dressed vacationers dining in the restaurant, or ambling by, or craning their necks between the rows of yachts to glimpse the private quarters of the rich – in the midst of the happy chatter around him and the pleasant sounds of cutlery on plates and the tinkling of wine glasses – with Charlotte on one side of him, and his father on the other, and Kathy seated across the table looking full of compassion – in the midst of all this he had never felt lonelier, never sensed such an agony of failure. Still, he made no move to pursue Bart through the crowds.

Charlotte started to rise. "Maybe I'd better go."

"No," Hershy said, "absolutely not!"

"But he's liable to take off," Charlotte protested, "and God only knows where we'll find him."

Hershy was adamant. "I am finishing my dinner," he declared. "If he goes he goes. It's his problem now." As they resumed eating, Hershy said to Kathy: "I'm sorry about all this ... Believe me, normally we don't make a habit of dragging strangers into our family swamps."

"Don't worry, I'm used to Bart," Kathy smiled. "Many of our talks together end up with a lot of door-slamming and the landlady gets very upset."

"Whose landlady," Hershy asked, "yours or his?"

Kathy thought for a moment. She well understood the point of the question. Full of a sense of her own as well as Bart's decency, calmly looking Hershy straight in the eye, she answered: "I'd say it's a tossup, Mr. Brahms."

Hershy paused to absorb the answer. "Then I guess you've gotten to know each other – shall we say – extremely well?"

"Yes," she said, then turning to Charlotte she added, "I wouldn't be too concerned about Bart disappearing if I were you."

"But sometimes when he gets into a particularly alienated mood like that, he stays away for hours," Charlotte said.

A slight smile appeared on Kathy's face. Quietly, confidently, she said: "He'll be back soon."

Scarcely had she uttered these words when Bart appeared at the entrance to the restaurant and made his way to their table. Without a word, he sat down and dug his fork into a slice of veal whose sauce had cooled and begun to gel. "Could you pass the salt please," he said.

"Do you want the waiter to take it back and reheat it?" Hershy asked.

"Just the salt please," Bart said.

Hershy passed him both the salt and pepper, as if the handing over of the additional unasked-for condiment were a peace offering, or at least a modest token that a truce existed. Hershy felt that he could be generous; after all, Bart's unexpected return to the table was a kind of victory.

There was only one question in Hershy's mind, however: who had really scored the winning point, he ... or Kathy O'Hearn?

On the drive from Beaulieu back to Nice Hershy remained silent, lost in his own thoughts. What a setup for a kid of twenty: France ... a girl who's a few years older, just old enough to possess that extra touch of experience that counts, and certainly easy to look at, smart, polite, family's probably got the first Yankee dollar ever earned in Boston.

He thought of himself as Bart's age, trying desperately to make it with one Agnes Broughton, a nurse-in-training at Toronto General (nurses were the safest; they knew how to "take care of themselves") ... After six or seven fruitless Saturday nights in the back seat of Louis' latest Chrysler, Hershy abandoned his campaign with the impenetrable Miss Broughton in favour of a sure lay every couple of weeks with Doris (no last name) who lived in a comfortable duplex on Broadview Avenue and gave college kids a break at fifteen bucks a shot; or with Eleanor Rutherford who did it for nothing in any location ample enough to accommodate two horizontal humans. One night Louis looked up from his Jewish newspaper and spoke sternly: "Tomorrow, Hershy, you'll take the Chrysler into the Shell station and tell Mario to clean up the upholstery in the back seat it should look nice again."

'There's nothing wrong with the upholstery in the back seat," Hershy said.

"It looks like the First World War back there," Louis said, sterner than before. "I wasn't born yesterday,

163

Hershy. When are you gonna settle down, stop chasing shiksas all the time?"

"How do you know it's from chasing shiksas?"

"Because from chasing a nice Jewish girl you don't get footmarks and lipstick and God knows what else all over the back seat."

Louis Brahms was so jubilant the first time Hershy brought Charlotte Zimmerman into Glicksman's Hearth-to-Table that next day he promised his son a new Studebaker coupe with windows like an airplane, before the year was out. Soon after Hershy and Charlotte embarked upon four years of steamy petting in the Studebaker, on rec room sofas and occasionally in hotelrooms during football weekends, but never between the sheets until Hershy's fraternity pin on Charlotte's cardigan evolved into a one-carat diamond ring on her finger, and even then it happened only once – and clumsily, incompletely at that, before the magic words "man and wife" were pronounced by Rabbi Emanuel Shulman.

Perhaps Bart and Kathy's way made more sense. Perhaps Bart was to be envied. But the more Hershy thought about it, driving along the dark Corniche toward Nice, the more he felt stooped with anxiety. Did the kid really know what the hell he was getting himself – getting all of them for Godsake – into? He envisioned a letter arriving from Bart: "Kathy's pregnant ... please forward funds care of American Express Stockholm." Or a headline in the social page of a Toronto daily: BRAHMS-O'HEARN NUPTIALS CELEBRATED IN BOSTON CATHEDRAL. Maybe the kids would do everybody a favour, reduce the pain a little for all sides: BRAHMS-O'HEARN NUPTIALS CELEBRATED IN UNITARIAN CERE-MONY. He envisioned Dr. Brendan O'Hearn of Beacon Hill seated at his first-ever Passover table, nibbling politely at his first-ever piece of unleavened bread, commenting to his Jewish hosts in broadest aristocratic Beaconese: "So this is what your people call mah-tzoe ... very interesting, very interesting indeed ... hmm." Perhaps the scales would tip in the other direction and Hershy would find himself at Bart's and Kathy's Christmas dinner, gagging on "Adeste Fideles" while the grandchildren – all eight of them for Chrisake! – ripped their presents to shreds under the tree.

Hershy allowed a groan to rise from deep within himself, but stifled it in his throat lest it escape and thunder against the steep cliffsides that lined the route along the Corniche. "Brahms-O'Hearn Nuptials ..." He thought about it. "Oh God no," he said to himself, "I'm not ready for that. Come and see me twenty-five years from now and maybe we'll talk it over ..."

Better still, he thought, fifty years from now ... there's plenty of time.

But there wasn't ... and Hershy Brahms knew it.

Kathy was dropped off at her room in Cimiez and Bart accompanied his family back to the Hotel d'Albion. Charlotte and Louis declined Hershy's offer of a before-bed Perrier and departed for their rooms, leaving Hershy and Bart seated on a bench where the front lawn met the sidewalk. Bart lit a cigarette.

Hershy screwed up his nose. "God those French things smell awful!"

"You don't like France very much, do you?" Bart said.

"No, not very much." What was there to like? The record thus far: two nights spent in rooms whose furnishings might have been rescued from somebody's grandmother's attic; airless, restless nights devoid of the slightest breath of romance. Where was France of the travel posters, the France of shaded parks and tree-lined rivers? Where was the other – the artificial – France, that extravagantly concocted creampuff inhabited by whispering lovers? Had the real and the unreal been wrapped and laid away in cold storage to prevent fading and melting under the rays of this hottest of July suns? Was there nothing for the likes of Hershy Brahms except traffic? Hershy ached, thinking to himself that France would come and go in his life, and in Charlotte's, and that all the senses that were theirs to fix upon this place would not be aroused beyond a kind of half-awakening. Then, feeling disgusted at his self-pity, he forced a smile and said: "It's probably not the country's fault. Maybe it's me." He chuckled. "Nerves."

"Nerves" – the simplest of all diagnoses, and the most vivid in his narrow range of medical experiences. Once again he heard the hushed cautions of his childhood, saw the anxious fingers pressed to lips ... "Mustn't upset your mother Hershy, her nerves are bothering her ... Don't disturb her this morning, it's her nerves ..."

"What's wrong with your nerves?" asked Bart.

Hershy chuckled again. Of course there was nothing wrong. Anyway, Hershy didn't believe in "nerves" as a diagnosis, anymore than he believed in leeches as a remedy.

Bart blew a perfect smoke-ring, so perfect and tight it held its shape almost all the way across the sidewalk before wobbling apart. At last he said: "Then I guess it's just that you're pissed off with me, right?"

Choosing his words carefully, Hershy replied: "Not pissed off Bart ... but concerned."

"You really mean worried."

"Okay, worried."

"About me and Kathy?"

Hershy nodded yes.

Bart's manner turned crisp again. "It really bugs you that I'm doing my thing this summer, doesn't it, Dad?"

"You kids kill me with that 'doing my thing' routine," Hershy said. "You make it sound like a crusade of innocents in search of beauty and truth, when in fact it amounts to staging a summer festival of sex. What else can you call it? Good God, Bart, Europe was meant to be something more in your life than that. I wonder if you truly appreciate how lucky you were to get this trip. When I was your age, if I'd announced I wanted to spend a whole summer in Europe my father would've driven his Chrysler into my legs."

Bart said: "If Kathy O'Hearn was some Jewish princess from Forest Hill you wouldn't be so uptight. You'd say terrific son, bang away to your heart's content, just so long as she's Jewish. Maybe Kathy O'Hearn's an R.C. but she's also the first person I've met in a long time who's made me feel like joining the human race again."

"In other words, your reunion with the human race is tied to a skirt," Hershy said in a voice heavy with sarcasm, "the skirt of an Irish Catholic yet!"

"I really resent this line of bullshit, you know," Bart said, becoming livid. "I suppose you'd be happier if I just sat in my room at night and read Voltaire?" Bart gave his cigarette butt a fierce flick into the street. After a moment of tense silence he said bitterly: "I guess I made a mistake at the restaurant. I shouldn't have come back, I should've kept going."

"Why the hell did you come back?" Hershy demanded.

Bart stood and faced Hershy, his hands on his hips. "I came back," he said slowly, "to prove I was a better man than you." The young man paused, dropped his hands to his sides and, looking strangely weary for his years, said quietly: "It's pretty late. I better be heading home."

Quickly Hershy got to his feet and reached for Bart's forearm. "Wait ... wait a minute, Bart," he pleaded. Bart put his hands to his hips again, a signal that he was prepared to be patient, but that time was running out.

"You want to be a better man than I am?" Hershy asked. "Fine. Great. But clear your head of these crazy dreams of yours and give yourself a chance." Hershy

167

looked intently into his son's eyes, eyes that were narrowed as if to strain out any bits of suspect advice. "You are going out of your way," Hershy went on, "to look for hard knocks in this world. I mean your infatuation with this get-rich-quick music business and getting mixed up with a girl whose background has nothing in common with yours. One fantasy in a person's life can be difficult enough to deal with. But two! ..."

Hershy paused, trying to discern from the look in Bart's eyes whether or not he was making any impression, but Bart's expression remained impassive. Almost coaxing now, Hershy continued: "Listen to me, Bart; be a better man than I ... learn at twenty what I had to learn so painfully at forty ... what your grandmother *never* learned ... cut out the fantasies, cut 'em all out, like bad weeds."

"You want me to cut mine out, while you go on having yours?"

"But I already told you," Hershy said, "I have none left."

"I'm afraid you overlooked one," Bart said with the air of a poker player laying down a trump card. "You have this dream of making me into a Xerox copy of yourself. That's your final fantasy. And it won't work, because I refuse to go into the machine."

Hershy stood on the sidewalk watching Bart mount his motorcycle and bring it to life. To Hershy there was something defiant about the kicking down of the starter pedal, the sudden roar of the engine. It seemed to Hershy that both cycle and cyclist had joined in a conspiracy to drown out – what? Hershy's ambitions for Bart? Or were those ambitions in reality Hershy Brahms' final fantasy?

Easing back the throttle, Bart said to Hershy: "Trust me." Then, gunning the motorcycle, he sped off in the direction of Cimiez.

Returning to his hotel room, Hershy found Charlotte asleep. That strange instinct that informs the sleeper someone is in the room awoke her.

168

"Hershy?"

"Uh huh." He stood staring out the window at the dark boulevard below.

"Aren't you coming to bed?"

Silence.

"Hershy?" Again silence. Charlotte slipped out of bed and went over to him. "Bart again?"

Hershy nodded, then turned and placed his hands firmly on Charlotte's shoulders. "Tell me something," he said, "do I look like a mink?"

Charlotte frowned, perplexed by her husband's odd query. Then, a little nervously, she smiled: "What on earth are you talking about, Hershy?"

"I'm serious Charlotte. I've never been more serious in my life. Do I look like a mink?"

Charlotte's smile faded, she looked confused again. "Hershy, are you ill or something?"

With sudden vehemence Hershy replied: "Yes, yes, godammit I'm ill ... sick to my stomach ... sick from the worst case of indigestion a man could have."

Alarmed, Charlotte asked: "Is it something you ate at dinner?"

"Yes, at dinner, and long before dinner. Something I've been consuming for a long time, Charlotte." He turned and faced Charlotte and she could see, even in the dim light from the bathroom, that his eyes were red-rimmed.

"What have you been consuming?" she asked. "And what's this talk about mink? I don't understand, you're not making sense, Hershy."

Hershy sat for a moment fighting back tears, attempting to suppress the well of sourness that was stored within him, sourness that had accumulated all evening when, in the midst of all the trappings of success he had so sharply come face to face with his latter-day failures.

"What's this talk about mink?" Charlotte repeated.

Hershy's voice was unsteady as he explained: "When I was a first-year law student, we had to study a line of negligence cases involving mink ranches. I think they

169

were mainly in the Maritimes ... maybe some were on the west coast as well. The ranchers were always hauling the airline owners into court, claiming damages. You see, during the whelping season, adult mink are especially highstrung and easily upset ... and every time a plane flew low over a ranch during a whelping season, the adult animals would be terrified by the noise ... and in their panic their first reaction would be ... to devour their offspring. A study was done on the mink ... on why they went after their own young in that fashion ... so blind, so destructive. Know what the conclusion was, Charlotte? Nerves. Nerves, for Chrisake! Now do you see what I'm getting at, Charlotte? I'm an adult mink ... in my whelping season ... and I'm eating up my own son. And it's nerves – Goldie Brahms' disease. I inherited all her diseases ... her daydreams, her nightmares—"

They continued sitting at the edge of the bed, and Charlotte held Hershy's hands between her own. They had sat like this once before – late on the night Charlotte had lost the election. On that occasion it was she whose eyes were red-rimmed and filled with tears, whose insides heaved with the bitter knowledge that she had been beaten by a lesser person, and it was Hershy who had told her over and over again how magnificent he thought she had been. They had made love then, the kind of slow, long love made when body and mind are exhausted. It was the tenderest moment they had ever shared.

Charlotte noted how bent Hershy suddenly appeared, how his shoulders drooped. All the building blocks of his personality, so neatly and strongly fitted together in his early forties, seemed suddenly to be separating.

"We're both in the whelping season, Hershy," she said softly. "It will always be the whelping season for us – you and me. That's why we've got to go home. Tomorrow. Not the day after or the day after that again, but *tomorrow*."

The light emanating from the bathroom was just sufficient to illuminate Charlotte's face. To Hershy her skin looked like fine suede, grown softer with age, more beautiful. Gently he laid his hand against her cheek. For a few minutes, there in the Hotel d'Albion in Nice, it was election night again.

The mechanics of checking out: opening and closing dresser drawers, peeking under beds, stashing away small unused cakes of hotel soap. Moral dilemmas for Hershy and Charlotte: to steal or not to steal a souvenir bath towel (what if the customs people? ...). Hershy eyes the bed. "Why don't we quietly tuck that away in your carry-on? They'll never suspect ..." he suggests to Charlotte. "Just take the mattress," she responds, "it'll fold in the centre." "I've got a better idea," Hershy says. "Why don't we just take the centre." Hershy does his Groucho Marx thing with his eyebrows. Charlotte smiles and gives him a peck on the cheek. They settle for a modest plastic "Cinzano" ashtray.

A pause at the window for a final look at the view. "Will we ever see boulevard Dubouchage again? ... Will that stone fence be here when we're dead and gone? ..." The scene is deepfrozen in the brain.

Louis, unlike the others, lugs his baggage along the lengthy corridor to the ancient creaking elevator and down to the lobby where he straightens his aging back and stands winded and perspiring from the effort (but pleased at saving five or six francs by forgoing a bellboy).

At the front desk, the handsome, correct, former military man presents the bill and hopes the guests had a pleasant stay. Charlotte, feeling cosmopolitan, replies "Merci et au 'voir." Hershy, whose mind is already aboard the jet winging westward, is determinedly North American: "Thank you ... hope to see you again."

At Nice airport a woman's voice echoes over the

terminal loudspeakers. Her voice, despite the hollowness of the sound system, is alluring, exotic. Hershy is certain she's describing in vivid detail an innovative new technique for love-making; actually she's announcing in French the imminent departure of a plane for Paris.

Bart had brought a small bunch of flowers. "Kathy says to tell you she's sorry she couldn't come. She has seminars till three every Wednesday." He handed the flowers to Charlotte. "These are from her."

"They're lovely, Bart. Thank Kathy for me. And tell her I'm sorry we didn't have a chance to say a proper goodbye."

"Me too," Louis chimed in.

Hershy drew Bart aside. Lowering his voice as always when the subject was finance, maintaining the illusion of strict confidence between father and son over the subject of dollars, Hershy asked: "How're you fixed for money, kid?"

"I'm okay."

"Could you use a little extra?"

"Honest, I'm okay, Dad."

Hershy was not entirely convinced ... or perhaps he didn't want to be convinced. This was one of the bonds between them and he wasn't ready to see it severed. "You'll let me know if you run short."

Bart, who hankered to see it severed, and dreamed of the day he could hand the keys of his new Ferrari to Hershy ("Go ahead, try it, Dad, but for Godsake watch out when you get her into second."), nodded reassuringly. After a brief moment of silence, Bart asked: "I still don't know the real reason you're leaving so soon. Mom said you were planning to stay a few days."

"Like I told you on the phone," Hershy said, "I remembered that I've got an arbitration hearing next week in Ottawa and —"

"I said the *real* reason," Bart broke in.

Hershy studied Bart's face. The sly smile on his son's countenance informed him that he might as well have pleaded a hundred arbitration hearings in Ottawa; the excuse would have been just as implausible. "All right, Bart," Hershy said, "let's just say I've gotten an urgent message to return to my frontier."

"You mean that mysterious Jewish outpost you couldn't bring yourself to talk about last night?" Bart said, still smiling, and feeling, despite the talk of monetary aid a few moments earlier, as if they were speaking as newly-created equals.

The voice of the French seductress came over the loudspeakers again. "They're boarding in ten minutes," Charlotte called to Hershy. He ignored the information. "Listen Bart, we don't have much time," he said, "and I don't know that I can make much sense in the next few minutes, but I'm going to try, because I owe it to you."

"You don't owe me anything."

"Yes I do," Hershy said. "The ball was in my court last night – you put it there – and instead of returning it, I threw the racquet at you like a damn fool and walked away."

Apologies embarrassed Bart; he found them difficult to offer, and just as difficult to accept. "It's okay," he said, "honest . . . let's forget it."

"Oh shit! It's not your willingness to forgive and forget that I want – it's your understanding. Forgiving and forgetting will get us nowhere." Hershy looked deep into Bart's eyes, noting that, unlike the night before when they were narrow with suspicion, they were open now, receptive. "My frontier," Hershy went on, "is the frontier faced by any man who takes the trouble from time to time to examine his life . . . except that mine's got a double set of hazards. When you start to push fifty, you take stock of all the things you thought you'd got taped, nailed down and arranged in alphabetical order during your forties, and suddenly you look closely and damned if things aren't beginning to warp and come unstuck, and you say to yourself oh God Almighty no! here I go again. And that's bad enough—" Hershy paused for emphasis, then continued: "But the extra set of built-in hazards involved in that kind of examined living comes from being a Jew. Because now that I've been to Israel I've got to make accommodations for that country in my life even though I choose to go home to Toronto and spend the rest of my days there, and even though I know that Israel will be a source of irritation as much as exhilaration. And I've got to deal with the possible existence of the Kathy O'Hearns in my life. And Canada or no Canada, I've always got to keep my ear tuned for the possible siren in the middle of the night and the gun-butt pounding on my door ... And I've got to hope that somehow ... by some miracle of pollenation ... the seeds of how I feel about being a Jew will land on you; but if they don't – well, we'll have to learn to live with that too, I suppose—"

Louis called: "Hershy, it's time!"

"In a minute," Hershy replied. "You and Charlotte get a place in the line; I'll be right there." He turned back to Bart. "I know you look at me, Bart, and say 'There goes a predictable man.' But if I were to drop dead at this very moment, I would leave all sorts of unanswered questions in my mind and in your mind. The unanswered questions are my frontier, Bart ... and they'll be yours before too long."

Not another word was exchanged between Hershy and Bart. There were quick fond embraces from Charlotte and Louis, and a long embrace from Hershy to which Bart surrendered totally, surprising both his father and himself.

Lingering final waves goodbye ... then Charlotte, Hershy and Louis turned and disappeared through the departure gate.

At Charles de Gaulle airport, outside Paris, they retrieved their bags. "We've got half an hour," said Hershy, checking his watch with the airport clock. "Just enough time to make the connection for Toronto."

174

Hershy noticed that Louis had set down his suitcase and flight bag. The older Brahms was mopping his forehead and there was an evident air of uneasiness about him. Worried that all the recent travelling about from place to place had finally caught up with his father, Hershy reached for Louis' suitcase. "You take your carry-on, Dad. I can handle this bag."

"Just leave it, Hershy."

"Really," Hershy insisted, "it's no trouble for me." He gripped the handle of the suitcase and hefted it under his arm as adroitly as any well-trained porter.

"Put it down a minute, Hershy, will you —"

"But we'll be late."

"*Please* ... I got to tell you something."

Hershy set down the suitcase.

"Are you feeling okay, Dad?" asked Charlotte.

"I feel fine. Never felt better."

"So?"

Louis took a deep breath. "Look, I'm not going back with you. I'm staying on in Paris a few days ... maybe a week or so."

Hershy spun around on his heels, doing a complete about-face in a release of tantrum energy. "Jee-sus Christ, not again!"

"Dad," Charlotte said, attempting to be patient, "I thought we went all through this once before. Can't we make you understand —"

"Charlotte my dear, there's a lot right at this moment that we can't make each other understand. Maybe later, after I come back home, we'll be more sucessful. The fact is, I'm not ready to go back to Glicksman's Hearth-to-Table and to Yoshke. That couple of days we were in Paris ... before we went to see Bart ... well, I just got to see it all again. And more."

"But how will you get around?" Hershy argued. "It's dangerous as hell on the streets. You saw it yourself, they treat pedestrians like flies!"

Louis brushed off his son's plea. "So every time an ambulance goes by I'll look to see who's in it, and if it isn't me, I'll know I'm all right for another little while."

Exasperated, Hershy barked at the old man: "Okay okay, I'm fed up. I've had it up to here. You want to be on your own, Dad? Fine, good luck. I've left a son; I can leave a father. But I want you to know ... from now on I'm absolutely positively no longer responsible ... for him *or* you!" Hershy paused to let this sink in, then added quietly: "You better take my moneybelt. That wallet of yours is about as discreet as a billboard."

Louis complied; if taking the moneybelt would make Hershy happy, then take it, he thought. Why cause the kid further aggravation?

Charlotte asked: "Have you even got a place to stay?"

"I took care of that already," Louis said. "Look here ... I wrote down everything on this piece of paper. You'll make a copy for Yoshke, don't forget —"

Louis Brahms handed his son a slip of paper. On it he'd printed in careful block letters:

No. 5 RUE CHOMEL
TELEPHONE 548-35-53

"That's just an address and phone number," Hershy said. "Hasn't it got a name?"

A wistful expression came over Louis Brahms' face – that face fashioned in Russia, matured in Rumania, lined and leathery from his years in Canada, and recently scorched under the incandescent suns of Israel and southern France.

"The name you'll remember easy," Louis said. "It's called Hotel Lindbergh."